THE CITY IN THE GLACIER
The War of Powers: Book Two

THE TREASURE: a magical amulet that brings the dead back to life. The quest: Stay alive long enough to find it.

Somewhere in the frozen depths of a living glacier lies a magical city, and somewhere in the city is the amulet. Only Erimenes, a crafty genie, knows the path inside. But his intentions, of course, are less than honorable.

Traveling with him are the lusty Fost Longstrider and his lover, the Princess Moriana. With the amulet, Fost's adventures could never end. But the princess needs it in her battle to regain her throne against the treachery and magic of her evil sister Synalon.

And let us not forget the lovable Prince Rann, who could happily flay the skin from your bones just in time for lunch. The prince has been charged by Synalon to bring back the amulet, or else. And we all know what that means.

THE WAR OF POWERS

THE WAR OF POWERS SERIES

THE CITY IN THE GLACIER

ROBERT E. VARDEMAN
AND VICTOR MILÁN

PLAYBOY
PAPERBACKS

For Carrie, who's earned it
—vwm—

For my parents, with love and gratitude
—rev—

A Chronology
of the Sundered Realm

—20,000   The reptilian Zr'gsz settle the Southern Continent and begin construction of the City in the Sky.

—3,100   Istu sent by the Dark Ones to serve the Zr'gsz as a reward for their devotion.

—2,300   Human migration begins.

—2,100   Athalau founded by migrants from the Islands of the Sun.

—1,700   Explorers from the Northern Continent found High Medurim.

—1,000   Tension increases between the Zr'gsz and the human settlers.

—31   The Zr'gsz begin active campaign to exterminate all humans.

—3   Martyrdom of the Five Holy Ones.

0   *The War of Powers:* Unable to wipe out the human invaders, the Zr'gsz begin to use the powers of Istu. Most of the Southern Continent is desolated. In Athalau, Felarod

7

raises his Hundred and summons up the World-Spirit. Forces unleashed by the struggle sink continents, tip the world on its axis (bringing Athalau into the polar region), cause a star to fall from the heavens to create the Great Crater. The Zr'gsz and Istu are defeated; Istu is cast into a magical sleep and imprisoned in the Sky City's foundations. Conflict costs the life of Felarod and ninety of his Hundred. Survivors exile themselves from Athalau in horror at the destruction they've brought about.

Human Era begins.

100   Trade between humans and the Zr'gsz grows; increasing population of humans in the Sky City. Medurim begins its conquests.

979   Ensdak Aritku proclaimed first Emperor of High Medurim.

1171   Humans seize power in the Sky City. The Zr'gsz are expelled. Riomar shai-Gallri crowns herself Queen.

2317   Series of wars between the Empire of Medurim and the City in the Sky.

2912–17   War between the Sky City and Athalau; Athalau victorious. Wars between the City and Athalau continue on and off over the next several centuries.

5143   Julanna Etuul wrests the Beryl Throne from Malva Kryn. She abolishes worship of the Dark Ones within the Sky City, concludes peace with the Empire.

5331 Invaders from the Northern Continent seize Medurim and the Sapphire Throne; barbarian accession signals fresh outbreak of civil wars.

5332 Newly proclaimed Emperor Churdag declares war on the City in the Sky.

5340 Chafing under the oppression of the Barbarian Empire, the southern half of the Empire revolts. Athalau and the Sky City form an alliance.

5358 Tolviroth Acerte, the City of Bankers, is founded by merchants who fled the disorder in High Medurim.

5676 Collapse of the Barbarian Dynasty. The Sky City officiates over continent-wide peace.

5700 The Golden Age of the City in the Sky begins.

6900 General decline overtakes Southern Continent. The Sky City magic and influence wane. Agriculture breaks down in south and west. Glacier nears Athalau. Tolviroth Acerte rises through trade with Jorea.

7513 Battle of River Marchant between the Quincunx Federation and High Medurim ends Imperial domination everywhere but in the northwest corner of the continent. The Southern Continent becomes the Sundered Realm.

8614 Erimenes the Ethical born. Population of Athalau in decline.

8722 Erimenes dies at 108.

8736   Birth of Ziore.

8823   Death of Ziore.

9940   Final abandonment of Athalau to encroaching glacier.

10,091   Prince Rann Etuul born to Ekrimsin the Ill-Favored, sister to Queen Derora V.

10,093   Synalon and Moriana born to Derora. As younger twin, Moriana becomes heir apparent.

10,095   Fost Longstrider born in The Teeming, slum district of High Medurim.

10,103   Teom the Decadent ascends the Sapphire Throne. Fost's parents killed in rioting over reduction in dole to cover Imperial festivities.

10,120   Jar containing the spirit of Erimenes the Ethical discovered in brothel in The Sjedd.

Mt. Omizantrim, "Throat of the Dark Ones," from whose lava the Zr'gsz mined the skystone for the Sky City foundations, has its worst eruption in millennia.

10,121   Fost Longstrider, now a courier of Tolviroth Acerte, is commissioned to deliver a parcel to the mage Kest-i-Mond.

CHAPTER
ONE

"If Rann's bird-riders don't kill us, this damned wind will. Doesn't it ever stop?" Fost Longstrider shouted over his shoulder. As if to mock his words, the wind died momentarily. A teasing lull, and then it blew full force again, hurling the eternal chill of the antarctic waste beyond the Rampart Mountains into their chapped, reddened faces.

His companion hunched closer, both to hear his words and to share his body's warmth. Numbed hands plucked ceaselessly at her heavy velvet cloak, tightening it against the cold in a gesture long since turned into reflex. The woman's fingers were long and fine, unmarked by labor save for the small, distinctive calluses left by long hours spent wrapped about the hilt of a sword.

"I thought you were used to living in the wind and weather," Moriana shouted back, blinking as the blast whipped her golden hair painfully into her eyes. "I thought you couriers spent all your time out on the road."

"I thought you princesses spent all your time lolling about in jewel-encrusted towers on satin pillows and thinking about how best to gratify your every whim."

Moriana managed a short laugh. "I suppose we've still a lot to learn about each other."

"In the old days," a third voice said, "the weather was worse. The wind blew harder and colder, the snow lay deeper when it came, and for months out of the year the sun never rose at all this far south." The thin, plaintive voice issued forth from a bulky knapsack slung over the courier's back.

"Come, Erimenes," said Fost. "You don't expect us to believe such wild stories."

13

"It's true," the voice insisted. "It was quite some time ago, of course. Long before my birth, to say nothing of my death. During the War of Powers ten thousand years ago, it was, when Felarod and the Earth-Spirit challenged the might of the Dark Ones. The struggle tipped the world on its axis. It brought these once fair and temperate lands into the icy grasp of the south pole and sealed the fate of lovely Athalau. I would not lie to you."

"Oh?" said Fost, in mock surprise. "Has the cold caused such a drastic change in your character?"

"Scoff, lowborn," sniffed Erimenes. "I tell you nothing but the truth."

Fost nodded, inclined to believe the spirit this time, yet unwilling to allow Erimenes the opportunity to gloat. In the vast libraries of High Medurim, Fost had read of a cataclysmic struggle in the distant past. But being born in the worst slums and learning the treacherous ways of the capital of the once-great Empire had turned him into a bitter realist. He had dismissed the tales as fantasy, mere legends concocted by the romantically inclined to add spice to the otherwise dreary march of history. He had forgotten the tales until just a few days past, when the honey-haired daughter of High Councillor Uriath of the Sky City had entertained him with the history of that ancient community.

Now he wondered how much truth was contained in those ancient tomes. Yet his hardheaded approach to reality refused to yield totally in spite of his recent confrontations with fire elementals, ape-monsters that ran through walls like wraiths but whose talons tore flesh like steel hooks, and idols that came to life imbued with the souls of sleeping demons. Abruptly he threw back his head and laughed into the teeth of the wind.

"Are you taken insane?" asked Erimenes hopefully. "Might I expect some new and diverting escapade from you?"

"It's nothing, old spirit," said Fost, wiping away a tear before it turned to ice on his cheek. "It just occurred to me how absurd the universe really is. Here I am tramping across the Southern Steppe beside the sorceress-princess of a city that floats a thousand feet in the air, and riding in the satchel at my hip is the spirit of a philosopher who has died fourteen hundred years before. . . ."

"Thirteen hundred and ninety-nine," corrected Erimenes haughtily. "Get your facts straight."

"And," Fost continued, as though the wraith hadn't interrupted, "this bizarre trio is bound for a city lost in the bowels of a glacier, in search of a talisman that confers the blessing of eternal life."

"All you ever think about is that amulet," complained Erimenes. "One would think there is nothing else in the world."

"Isn't eternal life a worthy enough goal, Erimenes?" asked Moriana.

"Yes, laugh, ridicule my warning to snatch at all the experience you can now. Mark my words. This fool's errand to retrieve the amulet will only earn you death, not eternal life," Erimenes said sourly. "Right now the journey is easy. You'll find it otherwise when Rann catches you and starts winding your guts onto a spool before your eyes."

"You'd like that," said Moriana with sudden savagery. "It would be quite a thrill for you to watch, wouldn't it? I don't doubt you'd stand by and offer helpful suggestions as you did when I was captive and my eunuch cousin forced me to watch him torture to death the friends of my childhood."

Fost gripped her shoulder. Moriana's face had gone white. Her capture in the Sky City had left scars on her soul that even time might not obliterate. She had returned to the Sky City to find her beloved mother dead and her hated sister usurping the throne. Within hours she was a prisoner, trapped by her cousin Rann's secret police. And at Synalon's command, Prince Rann had refrained from tormenting the prisoner—physically. He had found other ways of torture, ways leaving her body unsullied for her sacrificial marriage to Istu, the Demon of the Dark Ones.

Black Istu slept in the foundations of the Sky City, bound there at the end of the War of Powers by a victorious Felarod. For centuries the humans, who had supplanted the reptilian Fallen Ones responsible for building the City thirty millennia before, had sacrificed select members of the Blood Royal to Istu, in the form of his Vicar, an obscene stone statue that squatted at the City's core. Though Istu slept eternally, his subconscious remained active with a primitive, elemental life. This force could be drawn into the Vicar by the arcane chants of the Rite of Dark Assumption. For a time after the chant, the stone would pulse with unholy life —time enough for the demon to consummate his union with his latest victim.

Five thousand years before, Julanna the Wise had overthrown the necromancer Malva Kryn and founded the Etuul line. Her first act had been to suppress the Rite and all worship of the Dark Ones.

"Rann tortures only mind and body," continued Moriana bitterly, "but this is nothing compared with Synalon. My sister strives to serve the Dark Ones again after all these years."

"Don't let Erimenes goad you into argument," cautioned Fost. "He craves excitement. These dreary steppes are boring to him—and they are getting to me as well." He glanced at the blond woman and felt a lump forming in his throat.

Fost had rescued Moriana from Synalon and Rann, but it had been no mere altruism that prompted him to take such insane risks. He had followed a beauteous thief who had robbed him in the night, made it memorable with her lovemaking when he caught her, and then stolen away before dawn with the jug containing Erimenes the Ethical. And Erimenes alone, who had dwelt in Athalau before the glacier engulfed it, knew the location of the Amulet of Living Flame.

Fost's first discovery upon entering the City in the Sky was that his nocturnal thief was no less than Princess Moriana Etuul and rightful ruler of the City. His second was that she had been captured by her sister. Fost had already encountered Synalon's men searching for Erimenes and knew how deadly confronting them could be. With Erimenes secreted somewhere in the Palace of the Winds, Fost's only hope of finding him lay in asking Moriana. He had been forced by circumstance to rescue her.

He looked at the woman who strode beside him with steps still long and sure despite the fatigue he knew weighted her limbs. She was tall, nearly as tall as he. Her slimness made her appear almost frail beside his brawny bulk, belying a tigerish strength and swiftness that had almost claimed Fost's life at sword point the night they first met. The exchange of sword thrusts had turned into an exchange of thrusts of a different nature, but Fost had never forgotten the coldness felt when he realized he faced an opponent his equal in skill.

Her eyes, bloodshot now from the wind, were green, brighter and livelier than his own of smoke-grey. She was fair and blonde and lithe; he was burly, tanned and weatherbeaten, with a face framed by an unmanageable growth of black hair. In appearance they were as disparate as their backgrounds.

But even that first night, Fost had sensed something in her, some strand that matched one in the skein of his own existence. When he had trailed her across the steppe, fought his way up to the Sky City and found himself caught between Rann's ruthless efficiency and the equally deadly ineptitude of anti-Synalon rebels, he had told himself over and over that self-interest was his motive. She had robbed him of the key to life everlasting; he had meant to have it back. But he had never been able to hide from himself that his interest in rescuing Moriana ran far deeper.

And after rescuing her and escaping on the back of her aged, faithful war bird, he had learned that she, too, felt a strong link between them.

Moriana sensed his gaze, turned her eyes to his, smiled. He smiled back and looked away. In the green pools of her eyes he had seen the same knowledge that haunted him. Each ever-harder step to the South carried them nearer the decision that could sever forever the bond between them—or end one or the other's life.

Only one could possess the Amulet of Living Flame and the immortality it gave.

Night descended like a dome of black crystal, shutting out both wind and light. The steppe lay still under the cold blaze of constellations. Small soft sounds rustled in the dead grass around them, but none came near. The lesser predators of the steppe had learned that the smell of humans meant danger. The greater stayed clear, kept at bay by Moriana's magic.

Despite the cold the night was beautiful. But with his usual perversity Erimenes chose to wax morbid as Fost and Moriana supped on gruel.

"Rann may concentrate his search farther east, as you say, Princess," he said, with an obsequious bow in Moriana's direction. When they had stopped for the night, Fost had yielded to Erimenes's pleas and uncorked his jar. Now the spirit rose from the broad mouth of the jug, a thin spire of glowing blue haze that grew and resolved itself into the figure of a man. Except for his complexion Erimenes appeared much as he must have in life: a gaunt man of medium height, high of brow and ascetic of feature, with a lordly prow of a nose that seemed designed expressly for peering down at those of lesser intellectual attainments. The spirit looked exactly what he was, one of the more renowned philosophers of a city famed for its savants. Only a certain gleam in his eyes and a few lines etched around his aristocratic mouth hinted that Erimenes the Ethical had undergone a change since departing corporeal life.

When Moriana did not respond, he turned his attention back to Fost. "Even so, you must cross the southernmost reaches of the steppe, and then cross the domain of the barbarians who dwell in the shadows of the Ramparts. They are known to be most inhospitable to strangers."

Fost rubbed his chin, wishing they had a fire. But even if they had possessed fuel for one, a rare commodity on the virtually treeless steppe, they would not have dared light it. An airborne observer could sight even a spark for miles.

"I've heard of them," he said. "Nomad warriors, insanely suspicious, feuding among themselves like the clans of the Highgrass Broad. I've never been this far south before—not much call to make deliveries in these parts. But it's said they ride all manner of outlandish creatures, bears and badgers and outsized goats. No fit mounts for civilized folk, not like a good war dog." He caught the look Moriana shot him. "Or giant eagles," he amended. "But that may be just campfire gossip. You know how couriers are."

"Don't mention fires," Moriana said, drawing closer. Fost grinned and put his arm around her.

Erimenes shook his head. "Never have I seen folk so eager to commit suicide," he said. "And two so young! A shame to die, with all your lives before you."

"You're an old woman, Erimenes," Moriana said, looking at him wryly. "I'm not afraid of any skin-clad savages, no matter how unorthodox their mounts. Fost is right; rumor is as fickle as a fire sprite. These nomads of yours are probably starving and as timid as mice." She shook back her hair defiantly. "And even if they're not, what of it? I'm a princess of the City in the Sky. What have I to fear from a passel of wretched groundlings? I mean . . ." She blinked, and her skin darkened in the starlight.

Fost laughed at her eagerness to correct herself. The Sky Citizens' disdain for those who dwelt beneath their feet had been obvious to him the instant he entered the City. During his short stay in the City, he'd become acquainted with their favorite derogatory term for their earthbound fellows.

"And what of the storms?" Erimenes asked, returning to his point like a dog to its bone. "The Ramparts bear the brunt of the antarctic storms, but it is fast becoming winter. How will you find your way when a white wall of snow blocks your vision past the tip of your nose? How will you find food, shelter?"

"We've food a-plenty, Erimenes." Fost held up the bowl he shared with Moriana. As always when uncovered, it magically brimmed with an infinite load of unappetizing, murky, thin porridge. Ebony filigreed with silver, the bowl had been part of Fost's meager loot from the keep of Kest-i-Mond, the mage to whom he'd been sent to deliver Erimenes some weeks before. Moriana wrinkled her nose. Though nourishing, the gruel lacked anything resembling taste.

"For shelter we can dig in," Fost continued, "and I have a tent when the ground gets too hard. By that point the storms will probably be severe enough to ground Rann's bird-riders so we won't have to worry about concealment."

An idea hit him. "I know Rann's Sky Guardsmen are proof against your sorceries," he said to Moriana, "but do you have any power over weather? If you can whistle us up some nice, low clouds, we'll have nary a worry about running into your cousin."

"I've some of the weather magic," she admitted, "but no vast amount. It is a field all its own, one requiring much study and certain affinities I lack. The best I can do is—how can I say it?—shape and expand existing weather patterns, harness forces already set in motion by nature or the gods. I cannot create a cloud, but if one appears nearby I can influence it. Likewise a storm."

"Excellent." Fost brightened. "There's usually an overcast in the morning. If you get started early . . ."

"I don't think you understand," Moriana said quietly. "My control over weather is imperfect. At this time of year, so near the Southern Waste, I wouldn't dare to tamper with a storm. If I tried to make it grow it would probably get away from me. We could wind up in twenty feet of snow."

"Oh."

"Doomed," Erimenes intoned. "A shame. A sorrow. A waste."

Moriana put her chin in her hand and stared at him in exasperation.

"You, Princess," the spirit said. "So lovely, so fine and noble of limb and face. What a pity such a vision of loveliness should be nipped in the bud."

"You're mixing metaphors, Erimenes," Fost said.

"And you, even if you are lowborn and something of a guttersnipe, you're not displeasing to the feminine eye, I should say. Those muscles, while they could be larger, are far from insignificant. Remember the adventures you've known with other ladies. Would you throw all that away? I remember sweet Eliska. . . ."

Fost shook the jug hard enough to disintegrate the vaporous being momentarily. Actinic sparks swarmed within the luminous cloud, dancing like agitated insects. Erimenes's face reappeared wearing an expression of supreme indignation. "That was an ungentlemanly thing to do," he sniffed. "Most rude."

"This is not the time to elaborate on my, uh, adventures," Fost said. He rested his hand on the jug, lightly but menacingly, to show the spirit that more of the same could be expected if he continued that line of conversation in Moriana's presence.

"Spoilsport," Erimenes pouted. He turned a sorrowful face to the princess. "Have pity on a poor, disembodied spirit," he said. "Turn back from this mad escapade. Don't leave me stranded to spend eternity on the steppe beside your bleaching bones."

"So that's why you're so set against us going south, Erimenes," said Moriana. "You're afraid we'll both be killed and leave you helpless and alone. There wouldn't be any more vicarious excitement then, my nebulous friend, would there?"

"My foremost concern is the welfare of you, my two best friends in all the world," the spirit said, sincerity ringing from his words.

"I'm sure," said Fost sarcastically. He eyed the spirit intently. He had the feeling Erimenes's reluctance to venture south depended on more than fear of being marooned.

The spirit looked keenly at him, then at Moriana. "You're still determined?" They nodded in unison.

He sighed. "Well," he said, "if you are committed to this folly, so be it. But since you have so little of life left, why not make the most of the time at hand?" A knowing leer marred the spirit's distinguished features. Fost sighed. Erimenes was up to his old tricks again.

In life Erimenes the Ethical had preached a turning away from all worldly concerns—and most especially the pleasures of the flesh. So great was the power of his mind, he maintained, and so total his otherworldliness, that on the death of his body his spirit survived to be immured in an Athalar spirit jug. But Erimenes's afterlife was blighted by a tragic irony.

Death had brought a revelation to the ascetic philosopher: The only worthy life, he decided after centuries in the jug, was one of utter hedonism, the only goal sheer physical pleasure.

Both of which it was now too late for him to enjoy.

He could, however, watch others live their lives and experience through them the sensations forever denied him. If those around him did not show what he considered a properly hedonistic outlook, he was quick to offer suggestions. At the best of times it made him a nuisance. At the worst, when danger loomed and his bloodlust was aroused, it proved perilous. Erimenes was indispensable to their quest for the Amulet of Living Flame and eternal life, but sometimes both Fost and Moriana wondered if immortality was sufficient recompense for putting up with him.

Something small and warm slipped inside Fost's cloak and into his jerkin. He looked down at Moriana. She smiled slowly and kissed him.

"It's cold out," she said, nuzzling closer. "And who knows? Perhaps tomorrow we will hear Hell Call. For once I think our friend's advice is sound."

"Since you put it that way . . ." Fost began. She stopped his mouth with hers.

And for a time the cold of night was banished.

The tenth day after their flight from the City, they reached the foothills of the Rampart Mountains. The Ramparts blocked off the huge ice-sheets and the bitterest cold of the Southern Waste, but the wind blew southerly, its tendrils seeking out every winding passage through the Ramparts to clutch at the travelers' limbs like frigid, insistent fingers. The night was simply too cold to be walking. Marching during the day had not pleased Fost at first. Should Rann have bird-riders on picket duty along the north face of the Ramparts, the arduous journey could come to a short, ugly end.

"If Rann comes this way he won't patrol this region with less than his full force," Moriana had assured him. "The thulyakhashawin lair in these mountains." The thulyakhashawin were winged foxes, the only flighted creatures in the Realm capable of meeting the eagles of the Sky City on equal terms in the air. Not bats but actually winged vulpine carnivores, the thulyakhashawin hunted in packs and attacked the Sky City birds on sight. This news had alarmed Fost as much as the thought of Rann finding them, and Moriana's assurance that the foxes seldom attacked humans afoot did little to soothe him.

"Well," he said, looking up, "we'll not be plagued by eagles or foxes today." The clouds hung dense and impenetrable, so low it seemed as if he could reach out and touch them. It was as if a fluffy white roof had been laid above the rocky hummocks that had begun to interrupt the steppe.

"Brrr." Moriana shivered and drew close to him as a gust of wind blasted into their faces. She wore her gold-lined maroon cloak, the one she'd left with Fost in the forest after robbing him of Erimenes. He had taken it from his sled along with the other gear, which now rode in a knapsack slung on his back.

Fost squinted into the wind, tears rolling down his cheeks. "That damned gruel doesn't do much to warm a body," he said. The cloud cover took his words and cast them back in a flat, ghostly echo. It was as if they had somehow stumbled into a gigantic hollow chamber.

"You've no one to blame but yourself," Erimenes said. "You insisted on coming this way against all my good advice."

"It's doubtless just as cold to the East," Fost pointed out. Erimenes lapsed into sulky silence. Fost sucked in his cheeks. At first he had relished Erimenes's lack of verbosity, but of late he'd come to share Moriana's suspicions. The spirit had displayed unexpected abilities at the fight back in the ravine. He was, after all, born in Athalau, though he had lived long after the heyday of that city. It was unlikely Erimenes would tell more of his powers unless it suited him, and Fost could think of no way to compel him. With one hand hugging Moriana close and the other holding his own cloak shut against the gelid wind, Fost put his head down and trudged on into the stiff gale.

They had walked for what seemed an eternity when the blizzard struck. The wall of white rolled over them like an avalanche. At first, blinking at it as the gusts stabbed his eyes like daggers, Fost thought it was the cloud that perpetually hung above the Great Crater Lake. According to Moriana a volcanic vent at the bottom of the lake kept it from freezing even in the deepest cold, and the steam that rose from the warm waters held heat within the crater like a lid covering a bowl.

"Look," he said, fingers plucking at Moriana's shoulder. "The cloud—we've made it!" Thoughts of sinking his half-frozen limbs in balmy water drove him forward. He broke into a run, dragging the princess with him.

He saw dancing motes of whiteness, and the snow swept over him like a tide. He cried out in disappointment, wiping the snowflakes from his face and watching them melt slowly on his palm. Moriana glanced up at him but said nothing.

He shook his head violently. The nervous strain and physical exhaustion of the last two weeks were wearing him down. The erosion of his strength and will could be as deadly a foe as the cold or the forces of the Sky City. "We should stop and try to ride the storm out," he shouted above the clamor of the wind. "It's death to keep moving through a blizzard like this."

Moriana shook her head. "There's no place to take shelter, and the ground is too frozen to dig in." She waved a hand to still his protests. "I know we could sit with our backs to the wind, huddling beneath our cloaks for warmth. But why delay what must be? All that could save us would be a fire, and we don't have any dry fuel. I'd rather meet my fate standing up—and fighting."

Erimenes spoke. The torrents of wind washed away his words. Fost's arguments died unspoken. *What difference does it make?* he asked himself. *If the storm subsides, we may have a chance. Otherwise we die, sooner or later. What do a few miserable hours matter?* He bent his head and walked on.

The snow mounted until they stumbled through deep drifts, their feet leaden. The cold leeched thought and emotion from their minds as it sucked the heat from their bodies. They moved through a white swirling fog that existed as much inside their skulls as without. Fost tripped over an unseen obstacle and fell. The wet bite of the snow on his numb face revived him for a moment. Moriana apathetically helped him to his feet. A few minutes more and the spark of life that had flared within him died until he was scarcely aware of who he was.

Knives stabbed up his calves at every step. He vaguely welcomed the pain as a sign that some life still lingered. His lungs burned. The force of the wind was like a river at full flood. It took all his dwindling strength to make headway.

The white hours passed, a waking nightmare of featureless, icy, surreal tapestry. A voice cried for him to stop, to sink into the snow and conserve what vitality remained. He ignored the voice within his skull and concentrated on the task of lifting one dead weight that was a foot and heaving it in front of the other.

What does it matter, what does it matter, what does it matter? The question thudded in his brain like slow blows of a mallet. Yet he also heard the words, *Listen to me, fool, I can guide you to safety. Curse you, you thickheaded clod of a courier, I can save you!*

He stopped short. Moriana plodded on a few steps and then sank to her knees. Cascading snow turned her instantly into a white statue.

"Erimenes?" Fost asked dumbly.

"By the bones of Felarod, yes!" The spirit's words rang inside his mind.

Am I imagining this? he wondered.

"Turn forty-five degrees to your right and proceed," the voice said. "You'll come to a gentle slope. Go up it until I tell you where to go from there."

Fost shook his head. He had aged millennia since the storm began. "Too tired," he said.

"You mush-brained lout, you'll be more tired soon. Your body temperature is dangerously low. If you lose much more heat, you'll experience eternal rest. And I shall be stuck in the midst of this eternal waste, watching two frozen bodies that instead could be intertwined in acts of fornication."

Fost blinked. "I could never imagine a statement like that," he said, shaking his head hard. From somewhere strength flowed into his limbs like a warm tide. His fingers, toes and nose began to sting as circulation returned. "Erimenes?"

"Yes, fool, I'm stimulating the flow of your adrenaline. But the effects will soon be gone, and then you'll be beyond my power to help. Get the princess to her feet and *move!*"

Fost struggled forward and shook Moriana's shoulder. Her head swung disconsolately from side to side. "Lost," she said. "We've lost the amulet. What shall become of my City?"

When a second shake produced no further result, Fost stooped, put his hands under her armpits and hauled her upright. She looked at him, green eyes glazed and dull. When he started walking, she went along without protest.

As predicted, the ground soon began to rise in front of him. Slick with snow, it offered little traction to his bootsoles, and he found himself and Moriana floundering along on all fours. When he blinked snow from his eyes to look at the princess, her pale face had set in determined lines. Apparently Erimenes had invigorated her as he had Fost.

The slope went on forever. The fresh vigor ebbed from Fost's brain and limbs, gradually at first, then rapidly draining until he felt as if his life seeped through his bootsoles and into the frigid ground.

Something jarred his knees. It took him a half-dozen heartbeats to realize he'd fallen to his knees on snow-sheathed rock. Even the jagged pain did not tear through the deadness that shrouded his brain.

"Up, up! A few more steps. I beg of you, Fost, stand up and walk!" The note of pleading in Erimenes's words roused Fost to action. Dimly he realized that for the shade to abandon his usual superciliousness was a significant event. He hoisted himself to his feet once more, though it seemed he carried the weight of all the Rampart Mountains on his shoulders.

"Erimenes," Fost gasped. "Where are you leading us? Don't toy with us. If there's not safety ahead, let us die here and now!"

"Onward," the spirit commanded. Fost obeyed. But his limbs were slipping from his control. His senses dimmed. The final weariness set in. Then there was no ground where he put his feet. He fell. And rolled.

A boulder stopped his headlong plunge. He raised his head and screamed as boiling air scalded his face. He covered his face with his hands. Live steam ate the flesh from his fingers. Shrieks of agony ripped from his throat as madness seized his mind.

Slowly the realization came to him. He was not being boiled alive. His nerves were only responding to the sudden onslaught of warmth.

Warmth! He dropped his hands from his eyes. Clouds still billowed around but they caressed with gentle, soothing, life-restoring heat.

He stood. He was alone. "Moriana!" he cried, his voice a raven's croak. "Moriana, we've made it. We've reached the Crater!"

Silence answered him. He peered about in the fog. Where was Moriana?

A slim figure approached through the swirling whiteness. With a happy cry, he slogged toward it. "Moriana!"

A puff of wind parted the mist that veiled the figure. Fost saw a face of unearthly beauty, of calm and sculptured features. But it wasn't Moriana's. A stranger's face, effeminate but clearly male, regarded him with quiet pity.

Fost toppled into darkness.

He woke with a familiar hand clutching his. "Moriana?" The name came out in a broken whisper. With prodigious effort he raised his head.

Lying on a pallet next to him, the woman nodded. The skin on her face had turned to parchment, stretched taut across her cheekbones. Yet for all her gauntness she was as beautiful as when first he'd laid eyes on her. More beautiful perhaps. He perceived nuances of feature and form, shadings of beauty in the planes and curves and texture of her face, that he had never before noticed.

He let his head drop back and slept again.

Delicious warmth bathed Fost's tongue. He raised his head, eyes shut, and felt the tingling warmth suffuse his body. The aroma rising from the earthenware bowl satisfied his hunger almost as fully as the rich, thick broth.

He opened his eyes. Moriana sat cross-legged on the other side of a low wooden table. She wore a robe of orange cloth inlaid with intricate whorls of red and silver that lay open in the front, revealing creamy slices of her breasts and a tuft of tawny hair below her belly. The sight filled him with desire, yet of a languid sort, not at all demanding.

Moriana's eyes gleamed like green gemstones. Love and serenity shone from them. Fost and Moriana raised their cups in a silent toast. The broth tasted like hearty meat stew and also like a fine liqueur. Fost found it both nourishing and intoxicating at the same time.

"Good," he said.

"You are welcome," said their host, entering the room and seating himself at the table. The man's nostrils dilated delicately to drink in the essence of his own steaming cup. "We have not seen outsiders here within our lifetimes. We seek to avoid the brutish hurly-burly of the outside world. Yet we are glad that you've come to us. You are an influx of clear, fresh water into a stagnant pond."

A single taper, which burned without flickering, lit the room. Fost glanced around, noticing that the steady, mellow glow illuminated darkly irregular walls of slag. The rock had been poorly cut and dressed, and chinks had been stuffed with moss the color of dried blood to keep out the questing fingers of the wind. Still, Fost found the chamber pleasing. He recognized a higher standard of aesthetics than he was accustomed to. He couldn't truly appreciate it but he saw enough to know he was in the presence of beauty.

There was beauty in his host too, though Fost normally didn't spend much time contemplating the perfection of the masculine form. As tall as Fost, though slimmer of build, the man reclined in a robe of the purest white. His hair was the color and texture of spun gold; cobalt eyes looked forth from a perfect face, aquiline and fine. His only ornament dangled on a silver chain around his neck. An oblong inset with a rectangle of jet, its workmanship appeared as crude as that of the stonework Fost had seen. In the contentment brought by the broth and the smoking incense cones set on the table, Fost perceived the inner beauty of it.

"Tell me," he said, pausing self-consciously, aware how harsh his voice sounded after his host's dulcet, quicksilver tones. "Who are you people? We had thought none lived here but the barbarian tribes of the steppes."

Their host smiled gently. "Perhaps the world has forgotten us," he murmured. "Just as well. Ah, would that we could forget." His eyes met Fost's. "What we are, and who we are, cannot truly be expressed in words; only abstract concepts that require years to comprehend are meaningful. But you may call us the Ethereals. And I am Selamyl."

"Ethereals?" Moriana's brow furrowed. She set down her bowl. "I've heard of you, though I thought the stories were more legend than truth. Aren't you the ones . . ."

Selamyl raised a slender hand. Moriana fell silent at once, a flush creeping up the column of her throat at the awareness that she had said something to perturb the man.

"Do not be embarrassed, sister. The past is immutable, and we cannot change our part in it. Yet we do dislike to hear it spoken of by others." He set his own mug noiselessly on the table. "Yes, we are the descendants of the Ten Who Did Not Die, the survivors of Felarod's acolytes who summoned the wrath of the Earth-Spirit."

He steepled his fingers on his breast, sighing heavily. "Though the evil our ancestors helped to curb was great indeed, it was only at the cost of further evil that they acted. After the deed was done, they couldn't bear to remain in Athalau surrounded by constant reminders of their guilt. They wandered for years, homeless. Eventually they came here, where a star dragged from heaven by the War of Powers wounded the earth. By that time they had come to realize that they couldn't escape what they had done, and that it was only proper that they should dwell here, reminded forever after of the destruction magic could unleash."

"You spend your time in contemplation?" asked Fost.

"For the most part we do. Each must take his or her turn doing small tasks around the village, building, repairing, helping glean food from the lake or raising our few summer crops. The barbarian tribes hold the lake taboo and do not trouble us." For a moment Selamyl sat with eyes turned inward. "It took years for our forefathers to find a direction that had meaning to them. Then one day fourteen hundred years ago and more, a man came among us whose wisdom reshaped our lives. Of Athalau he was, yet he turned away from the materialism that had infected the city since the War of Powers. With marvelous cogency he set forth the very tenets toward which generations of Ethereals had been groping. Denial—this was the essence of his philosophy; denial of the worldly, its temptations and its baseness."

"Wait," Fost said, "could you be referring to Erimenes? Erimenes called the Ethical?"

Selamyl's eyes glowed. "It is so!" he cried. "Ah, that saint of a man who walked among us. He left us, alas, and what became of him later has not been revealed to us, though our deepest thinkers have long theorized that he was bodily assumed into the Paradise that is A Gift, to dwell among the Twenty-three and the Five. For such was his holiness."

Moriana coughed. She seemed to be choking on her broth. Fost opened his mouth to tell Selamyl that his saint was back among them, but a sudden tightening in his throat squeezed off the words. He glanced at the satchel laying by his pallet. Now he knew why Erimenes balked at passing near the Great Crater Lake. To come among folk who followed his teachings of his earthly years would prove an excruciating embarrassment, to say nothing of a bore.

Selamyl rose. "Would you care to tour our village?"

he asked. "It's small enough, but adequate for our needs. Our healers inform me you're well enough to be up and around."

"I've never tasted anything like this," Moriana said, finishing her broth.

"Nor I," Fost agreed, rolling the last of his own around on his tongue. "When we sat down I was famished enough to eat a roast war bird whole, complete with rider. Yet the one cup has filled me."

"We do not gorge ourselves on vast quantities of food," the Ethereal said. "Rather we have learned to prepare dishes that satisfy the appetite in small portions. Long ago we learned that a growling belly served to distract our minds from higher thoughts."

They followed Selamyl into the daylight. He moved with a gliding walk, his sandaled feet seeming to skim the ground. Looking at him in motion, they felt themselves models of clumsiness.

The cloud-muted sunshine showed them a settlement of two-score huts, all of the same melted rock as the one in which they were housed. The streets were wide, the earth packed by many generations of slowly pacing feet. Ethereals paced them now, men and women of fragile, otherworldly beauty, who discoursed in quiet voices or simply thought. To one side several inhabitants labored inexpertly at restoring a roof that had caved in. The others ignored them, as genteel folk ignore one forced by circumstances to relieve himself in a public place.

The water of the lake caressed a beach on the outskirts of the village. Flat-bottomed boats plied across the water, ghostlike in the omnipresent fog.

"Are they fishing?" asked Moriana.

"But no!" exclaimed Selamyl, his face showing horror. "We wouldn't feed upon the flesh of any living creature. They gather edible weed that grows in great profusion in the lake. This forms the staple of our diet."

In the past Fost had always been partial to great steaming joints of dog or hornbull beef, washed down with oceans of black ale. Now the thought of consuming the flesh of a fellow creature stirred uneasiness in his stomach. He found himself pleased that the broth he had consumed contained no meat. He looked at Moriana and knew at a level beyond words that she felt the same.

Her hand gripped his. They smiled at one another. It was as if they were children discovering the vastness of the world. The gentle Ethereals had opened to them vistas of a reality neither of them had imagined existed.

Laughing, they followed Selamyl along the beach.

The first day Fost felt a few vagrant tugs of urgency to continue the journey to Athalau. They quickly diminished to nothing. The Ethereals were expanding his mind to realms beyond the mundane. Time ceased to matter.

He and Moriana joined the routine of the Ethereals' life. They sat in circles with the rest on the floor of the round temple in the center of the village, chanting meaningless monosyllables meant to open their minds to oneness with the universe. They attended a dance in which the dancers stood all but motionless for hours on end and learned slowly to read the infinities of meaning implicit in each minuscule gesture. They listened to music played on a stringed instrument that produced sounds both above and below, as well as within, the normal range of human hearing and came to appreciate the richness inherent in the unheard. They reclined on mats in the evening, breathing subtle essences from tiny phials and groping after truths.

When night came they made love in their hut, but

without the wild intensity that marked their earlier couplings. Instead they performed their sex in a detached fashion, almost as if the nearness and joining of the flesh in no way involved them but happened to someone else observed from afar. At times Ethereals watched them, but it didn't trouble them. Their hosts seemed pleased at the progress they made away from material concerns, and that approval warmed them more than any carnal sensations could.

Erimenes, of course, did not approve.

"You must understand," Fost told him one night after making love, when the audience of Ethereals had drifted away to their beds and perfumed dreams. "They have elevated mere sex to the level of art."

"Boring art," the spirit said.

"You fail to appreciate the nuances," Moriana chided him. "It's the same as with their dance. The tilt of the head, the gradual alterations of posture—these assume paramount importance. It's all part of divorcing oneself from the material."

"I don't believe it," Erimenes wailed. "A tilt of the head more important than a passionate thrust of the hips? Alteration of posture merits greater enthusiasm than a male organ thrusting into your sex? You're as mad as these whey-faced Ethereals!"

"Erimenes." Fost shook his head with the same mild reproof Selamyl displayed earlier when he had spoken of leaving the village. "Try to understand them. They have been kind and more than kind in sheltering us and in granting us the fine gift of their teachings. You of all people should appreciate their wisdom."

"I'm not people. I'm a spirit and I tell you they're trying to become as disembodied as I. They venerate death, which I assure you is not all it's cracked up to be. This is boring! *Boring!*"

Fost chucked sadly. He pitied Erimenes. That the

philosopher, once so wise, should himself become blinded by the illusions of the material world struck him as tragic.

"Moriana!" Erimenes appealed to the princess, who sat by fondling one of the small clay figurines the Ethereals devoted so much of their time to sculpting. "Get us away from here. These people will swathe you in wool and suffocate you. You're a lively wench, you hunger for life and all that it implies. Don't deceive yourself into believing they offer anything but death in the guise of life."

Moriana didn't listen. She laid the figurine down and took up a glass phial filled with yellowish liquid. She unstoppered the phial, drank of the fumes and passed the container to Fost.

The fragrance tickled his nostrils, as fleeting as a snowflake. His mind struggled to unravel the complexities of that one brief sniff. He reclined on his mat, letting the implications of aroma percolate through his consciousness.

At the back of his brain he felt a prickling. It was familiar somehow, and then he realized he had known a similar sensation as he struggled up the slope of the crater, when Erimenes had stimulated him through some mental trick. Fost was not stimulated now. Instead he ignored the feeling, concentrating on the fragrance until sleep claimed him. He dreamed he walked on clouds of light.

The education of Fost and Moriana continued. They worked at modeling statues of yellow clay and were rewarded by murmurs of praise from the Ethereals, though they knew their efforts were shoddy in comparison. Their turn came at the menial tasks that needed doing. Moriana worked making robes and Fost helped in shoring up a part of the temple wall that had begun to sag. His physical strength, immense by comparison to the Ethereals, enabled him to do more than all the other workers combined. He felt abashed by this, as though his bodily powers were a sign of some gross imperfection.

When the job was done, he went back to his hut. Selamyl, who was the chief instructor of the village, had given him a smooth blue stone and told him to meditate upon it. He sat on his pallet and began to eat a meal of stewed pods taken from the lake.

"It's not too late to see if any slop-jars have been left unemptied," Erimenes told him.

Fost stared dumbly at the satchel. "What are you talking about?"

"You seem to eat up the Ethereals' dung with relish. I thought perhaps a dollop might liven up your meal. You're a pig, and you rut with sows."

"Sows?" Fost blinked.

"What else do you call Moriana? She's got the habits of a pig and the smell also."

"You mustn't say such things about Moriana."

"Why not? It's true. In fact she's worse than a sow. She and Synalon were lovers, you know. That's why she feels herself debased when she lies with you. She wouldn't do so at all, but when the urge to rut comes over her, she'll couple with anything that moves and much that doesn't."

"Moriana," Fost growled, picking up the satchel. "You can't insult her—me!—like that. I'll—"

"You'll nothing. You're weak and useless. Moriana thinks you much inferior to Synalon. You only have one advantage over her in bed, and even that's not much to brag about in your case." The courier snatched Erimenes's jug from the satchel and squeezed it. His fingers tightened like steel bands around the neck of the jar, as though he could throttle the life from the taunting spirit.

"Fool! Ineffectual fool! You threaten me as much as you pleasure Moriana."

Fost reared back, holding the jug high over his head to dash it in fragments against the wall. A wave of dizziness passed over him, followed by nausea. He swayed.

"Well?" demanded Erimenes. "Are you going to do anything or just stand there looking stupid?"

"What's happening, Erimenes?" Fost asked. "I feel funny."

"Not half as funny as you look. But there—did the anger purge you of their spell?"

"Spell?"

Erimenes made a sound of disgust. "Go back to listening to sounds you can't hear and dining on kelp. You deserve no more, man who buggers pigs."

Fost fought down a fresh surge of rage and sat heavily upon the pallet. His thoughts felt unnaturally sharp, his vision almost painfully clear. He saw the rough walls, the poorly made table that tilted to one side, the bowl so irregularly formed that it could be no more than half filled without its contents slopping over the side. The pallid pods that lay inside seemed to glisten like toads' eyes, and the scent, which had seemed to him so tantalizing and profound, now reminded him of boiled paper. Even so, their odor was more appetizing than the whiff that reached his nostrils from the open latrine near the edge of the village.

He looked down at himself. The white robe he wore had crooked seams and a hem soiled with human excrement.

"Pig?" Erimenes said tentatively. "Must I go on? I learned some truly fascinating sexual insults back in the

Sky City. Would you like to hear them, or have you come to your senses?"

Fost set the jug down. "I'd like to hear them some day, Erimenes, but right now tell me what's going on. Did they drug us?"

"That was part of it. And despite their avowed distaste for magic, they've used some mental compulsions against you as well; Moriana might have noticed but she was brought here weakened and unconscious, and when she awoke she was already meshed in the snares of the Ethereals. But mainly the appeal of a life of indolence proved too much for you. You're basically lazy, Fost, as I noted right from the start. You run when you should fight. You stray from the most enticing women. You—"

"Enough of that, you bottle of flatulence! How long have we been here?"

"A week," said Erimenes, "during which time you and Moriana were the most stultifying company imaginable, save for our hosts themselves. Do you think I rescued you from the storm just so I could rusticate till the end of time among these pious humbugs? I wouldn't have guided you to the Crater if there had been any other choice."

Fost didn't hear him. He was on his feet, pulling his knapsack onto his back, then stooping to gather up the satchel and stuff Erimenes back inside.

"A week!" he shouted. "Ust and Gormanka, Rann will be here at any moment."

He strode from the hut. Heads turned to regard him with amazement. He walked purposefully to the tumbledown shack where Moriana worked at sewing alongside other dream-sodden Ethereals.

"On your feet, woman," he ordered. "We must get to Athalau."

The Ethereals recoiled at the name. "Athalau?" Moriana said. "But it is so far, so full of sorcery and evil. Sit beside me and think beautiful thoughts. Forget Athalau."

He slapped her. Fire flared in her eyes, but only for a moment. The listless mantle of uncaring dropped back and she smiled at him, a mother's smile for a wayward child. "We are wanted, Fost. We belong here."

"Don't you miss Synalon? Don't you wish you had her to play abed with you? And Rann—how is it with a eunuch, bitch?"

"What are you saying?" Her voice had a definite edge to it.

"Erimenes told me you were a pig who slept with her own sister. I denied it but I think I owe him an apology. He was right. You *are* a pig. In bed you're worse."

"I'm better than Luranni," she hissed.

"Don't bet money on it. She knows tricks you're far too stupid ever to learn. Stick to eunuchs from now on."

"Bastard!" The back of her hand slammed into his cheekbone. He fell backward over a worktable. Ethereals drew back, staring at him with round, uncomprehending eyes.

"Bastard I may be, but that's better than a whore."

She came for him. No longer the mild, vague acolyte of the Ethereals, she burned with fury and the urge to kill. It already felt as if his jaw were dislocated. The lethal purpose of her movements reminded him just what kind of exquisitely trained killer the princess was. He caught her wrist just before she delivered a chopping blow to his neck.

"I'll rip your worthless lungs out," she snarled, driving a fist into his short ribs. "I'll roast your shriveled penis over a pit and fling it to the dogs. I'll . . ."

Abruptly she went still, her free hand frozen in the midst of a two-fingered strike at his eyes. "Fost?" she said, her voice small and unsure.

"The Ethereals. They're trying to change us."

"Why?"

"The proselytizing urge," Erimenes said. "I can't fathom it now, though once I myself, I shamefully admit, fell prey to it."

— A shudder wrenched through Moriana's body, as if she were throwing off the last gossamer rope that bound her to the Ethereals and their fantasy.

"We must leave," she said. "Now."

They left the Ethereals cowering in the hut. The sound of Erimenes's voice coming from the satchel had thrown them into a panic. The presence of magic was something they'd always been taught to dread.

If only they knew who was in the sack, Fost thought. The idea made him throw back his head and laugh. It occurred to him he'd almost forgotten how. It felt good. Everything felt good again.

Their swords had been cast on the village refuse heap. They quickly reclaimed them. As Fost buckled on his sword belt and Moriana tied a sash around her waist to hold her own blade, a voice hailed them from the village.

"Why do you leave?" Selamyl asked. "This is paradise."

"This is a shabby, reeking collection of hovels. A paradise only to those who dream," Fost said. "We'll take reality, thank you."

"But you mustn't go! Don't let yourselves be caught in the webs of illusion you call reality."

Fost felt the gentle tugging at the corners of his mind. "It's you who weave webs of illusion, Selamyl, you and the rest of the Ethereals. You've snared yourselves in them." Ignoring the wordless plea within their minds, he and Moriana turned and marched toward the rim of the Crater.

Behind them an Ethereal wept for the first time in generations.

Light blazed far into the night from a thousand arched windows in the Palace of the Winds. Borne by puffing groundling servitors, ornate sedan chairs made their way along the public paths flanking the Way of Skulls. Inside the conveyances rode desperately frightened men and women. They'd been ordered to an extraordinary meeting of the Council of Advisors of the City in the Sky by Princess Synalon. It was none too certain that any of them would leave the Palace alive.

By ancient tradition the councillors met to advise the ruler of the City in the Council Chamber, tributary to the immense audience hall that filled most of the Palace's ground floor. To the councillors' chagrin the stewards who greeted them at the Palace's main door ushered them directly to Synalon's own room, in which she had installed the Beryl Throne. The stewards were, as always, self-effacing to the point of invisibility. The clanking Monitors in their leather and blackened steel armor, faceless within low-swept sallet helmets, marched several steps behind and were highly visible.

The princess sprawled insouciantly at ease on her ancient jeweled throne. Cosmetics had done much to cover the bruises and scratches left by her brush with death the day before. She wore a gown cut loose, the skirt consisting of ebony strips joined at waist and hem. The way she had arranged herself in the blue-green crystal chair of state revealed strips of gleaming, pale flesh. To appear before the High Council so scandalously attired was as calculated an affront as Synalon's choice of meeting place.

Even before they saw the princess, the councillors

recoiled from the harsh glare, the heat and the insistent rushing noise filling the chamber. Ten feet to either side of the throne stood a tall bell jar. The sinuous, semireptilian shape of a fire elemental writhed within each. Seeing them, the councillors exchanged fearful glances and moistened their lips with their tongues. Even more than the score of Monitors ranged behind the Beryl Throne, the salamanders represented the fearsome power by which Synalon ruled the City.

A tall man, portly and red-faced, his smooth dome of a skull fringed by a ring of snowy hair, moved deliberately to the front of the knot of councillors. The others gave way to let him pass. As high councillor it was his place to protest the cavalier treatment accorded them by the princess. Synalon watched him, a smile playing on her lips.

"Well, High Councillor Uriath, have you something to say to me?" she asked.

Eyes turned to the high councillor, some expectantly, some with an expression akin to fear. His eyes met the princess's for a moment. Then they fell away.

"We are honored to obey Your Highness's summons," he said, stroking his white beard.

"So," she said, her smile growing. "Anacil, have chairs brought for our esteemed advisors." Her chamberlain gestured to the stewards, who began bringing chairs into the throne room. The score of advisors took their seats before the princess like schoolchildren at the feet of their instructor. Councillor Uriath sat in the direct stream of Synalon's gaze and blessed the years of experience at bartering and intrigue that kept his face from revealing the turmoil that raged within him.

Synalon had reacted to the debacle of her sister's sacrifice in the Rite of Dark Assumption with a response as amazing for its alacrity as for its savagery. Within hours after a fire elemental, launched by members of an underground hostile to Synalon, had attacked the Vicar of Istu and driven it to berserk fury, halberd-armed Monitors were kicking down doors all over the City. Overhead the eagles of Rann's elite Sky Guard still patrolled the streets to quell any sign of resistance. Three score had been slain, twice that many herded to captivity in the Palace dungeons. Synalon's ostensible reason for the mass arrests was a hunt for the traitors who had engineered the attack that had resulted in the escape of her sister, the loss of Erimenes and the estrangement of the Demon of the Dark Ones. Yet with the cunning she had exhibited even as a child, Synalon was quick to use the fiasco as an excuse to round up known enemies who were otherwise too powerful to attack. She still had no clue as to the identities of those behind the assault that freed Moriana. Uriath knew that for a fact.

Tho high councillor wondered if Synalon might be playing a cat-and-mouse game with him, if she had learned of his involvement and only tortured him now. His stomach turned over at the idea.

Synalon looked from face to face. Her advisors squirmed like worms impaled on a thorn. She found it very hard not to laugh out loud. Guilty ones sat among these twenty, of that she was sure. Sooner or later she would sniff them out and deal with them in a suitably instructive way.

But not this night. She had on her mind a matter more pressing even than ferreting out dissidents among the Council.

"I have called you here to ask that you vote me recognition as queen of the City in the Sky," she said abruptly.

The councillors sat back as if struck. Uriath blinked rapidly, trying to assess the situation. At his back the others whispered to one another in agitation. Each was trying to avoid asking the question that must be asked. At length a middle-aged woman with grey-shot blond hair stood at the rear of the assembly.

"Your sister the Princess Moriana still lives, Your Highness," she said, stressing the honorific applied to a princess. "As the younger twin, she and she alone is lawful heir to the throne. With respect, how can we confirm you against all law and custom?"

Synalon paled. "Moriana!" she spat. "*Moriana!* How dare you mention the name of that slut, that traitor, that offal! She who slew our mother in order to hasten her inheritance. She whose escape from just retribution cost the lives of a dozen of my Guardsmen. A bloody-handed murderess many times over!

"The gods alone know what means may efface the stain left on the City's honor by the crimes of regicide, matricide and treason visited by my sister. Would you deepen the taint by placing her on the Beryl Throne?" She stared at the woman and dropped her voice to a husky whisper. "Do you endorse these crimes, Elura? Would you then see such sins rewarded with mastery over the foremost city of the Realm?"

For a moment the woman stood erect against the force of the princess's baleful gaze. The only sound was the hissing of the salamanders, rising and falling with inhuman cadences. In the shadows behind the throne the salamander light picked out eerie highlights on the breastplates of the Monitors.

Elura's face crumpled into a mask of despair. She knew her death warrant was signed already, no matter what she did or said. But her will broke before Synalon's fury like a dry twig in a storm. She lacked the strength for a final defiance, which would cost her nothing not already forfeited.

"I beg your pardon," she said unevenly. "You are correct, Your Majesty." And Councillor Elura sat down under the triumphant eyes of the woman she had just acknowledged queen.

"I've no wish to rush you into such a momentous decision," Synalon said, winding a lock of hair carelessly about one finger. "Feel free to debate this matter among yourselves. Pretend I'm not here." She smiled again, her face as ingenuous as a child's.

"Uh, I feel that will not be necessary," said Uriath. He swept his scarlet-sleeved arm in a gesture encompassing his fellow councillors. "The justice of your argument is undeniable. I am sure none of my distinguished colleagues has any further objection to granting your wishes. Is it agreed?"

No one spoke. Hesitantly a woman on Uriath's left nodded. The others quickly joined, bobbing their heads up and down in unison like a collection of marionettes.

"Very well," he said, rising to his feet. "It is unanimously agreed by the Council of Advisors of the most favored City that Princess Synalon shall forthwith be proclaimed Synalon I Etuul, Mistress of the Clouds, Queen of the City in the Sky." He knelt on the unyielding stone of the chamber floor. "All hail Her Majesty."

"All hail Her Majesty," echoed the other councillors.

"Dark Ones, but the witch is cunning," the High Councillor said above the brim of his goblet. "We had no alternative to proclaiming her queen. None at all."

He looked around for confirmation from the others gathered in the sitting room of his manner. Outside the high window the land slid by, dark and silent.

Several of his visitors nodded, more readily than they had nodded acceptance of Synalon's request. Another, one who had not been present at the Council meeting, stood by one wall, staring reproachfully at Uriath out of large golden eyes.

The man saw the look and shook his head. "Luranni,

dearest child, you don't understand," he said, his voice heavy with paternal concern.

"I understand that you pledged to resist Synalon to the last drop of your life's blood," she said, scowling furiously at her father. "Now you've proclaimed her queen and you look remarkably pleased to me."

Uriath's three fellow councillors began to study intently the carved wood screens hung around the walls. Uriath frowned, then smoothed his face into conciliatory lines.

"Luranni," he said, "you are intelligent and perceptive for one so young. Otherwise you would not occupy a position of such responsibility in our family business. But still, there is much to be said for the wisdom only experience and age can bring."

Luranni folded her arms beneath her breasts.

"She held the whip hand, so to speak, and she made sure we knew it. A roomful of Monitors and a pair of captive salamanders no less! Our beloved sovereign was telling us in no uncertain terms that if we didn't accede immediately to her wishes, none of us would ever see the outside of the Palace again." He sighed, then drained his cup and held it up over his shoulder. A servant glided forth from a niche in the wall and refilled it.

"It was unsubtle, of course," Uriath continued, sipping wine. "Terribly unsubtle. Rann would have handled it differently, mark you. But the princess's—excuse me, the queen's—castrated pet is busy preparing the pursuit of Moriana and her courier."

"Our rightful queen!" flared Luranni.

Uriath licked his lips. "Of course. Our rightful queen." He waved a carefully manicured hand. "But if Synalon lacked her deadly pet, she had his shadow at her side. Colonel Chalowin of the Sky Guard. He hovered by her elbow like a nervous familiar spirit the whole time. Another manifestation, you see, of the power Synalon wields against us. *Now* do you understand, my child?"

Luranni turned her face away. Lamplight glinted in her hair like a cascade of honey. It was a peculiar, heatless light, emanating from a crystal filled with clear liquid set on the table around which Uriath and the others sat. It was filled with luminous beings, invisibly tiny, which when agitated gave forth the yellow glow. It was a less satisfying illumination than torchlight. But the mages of Rann's security network controlled captive fire elementals, using them to peer into any nook or cranny of the City illuminated by firelight. No flame produced this light, though, and so it was safe.

"We must be circumspect, my child," said Uriath, allowing a precise measure of exasperation into his voice. "One misstep and Synalon will destroy us all."

"One misstep?" His daughter spun to face him. To his surprise he saw the bright trails of tears down her cheeks. "What about the way your men failed to help Fost Longstrider rescue Princess Moriana? He was almost killed. Wasn't *that* a misstep?"

Uriath started to reply, collected himself visibly. "Why, ahh, yes, I suppose it was." He kneaded the doughy flesh of his cheeks. "Yes, it definitely was a mistake. But accidents can happen, my dear, keep that in mind. All the more reason for caution now."

Without a word the girl turned and stalked from the room.

Later Uriath sat in the sitting room, his only company a fresh bottle of wine. A soft chime roused him from his contemplation.

"Come in."

His chief steward opened the door, announcing, "A visitor." He seemed unruffled by the lateness of the hour.

Uriath turned to look out the window. A white turmoil danced outside: snow. He gestured for his servant to admit his visitor. A moment later he heard a footfall on the carpet behind him and the quiet closing of the door.

"Chiresko," he said. "I am disappointed in you."

"I am sorry, lord. I make no excuses. Failure cannot be excused."

Uriath sighed. Fanatics were such a dreary lot. "I appreciate your honesty. You've no idea how tiring it is listening to people whine about how it isn't their fault they didn't do what they were supposed to. But I'm still deeply interested in discovering what went wrong."

"I ask for no pardon."

"Thank you, Chiresko. You may dispense with the protestations. I require only facts."

He turned around to behold a pale youth with bright, bloodshot eyes and a shock of black hair. His intensity and sallow complexion reminded Uriath of Colonel Chalowin, and Chalowin had always made Uriath nervous. Still, Uriath was a businessman and knew he had to make the most of the resources available to him.

"I do not know, lord," he said slowly, trying to erase the perplexed look on his face. "The confusion was all you could have asked for. We waited at the distance you ordered. When the time came to make sure things went properly, there were too many people between us and the Skywell. That groundling was more a man than I thought; he had Princess Moriana away from the altar and into the crowd before anyone could react. And Rann, damn him, bought Synalon the time she needed to dismiss Istu's spirit from his Vicar." He scratched a boil at the side of his neck. "What I don't see, lord, is why we were supposed to prevent . . ."

"Enough," Uriath said sternly, raising his hand in a peremptory gesture. "It's not for you to see. It's for you to obey. That's how you serve your cause. Or do you doubt the sacredness of our mission?"

Chiresko stiffened. "Never!"

"It is well." Uriath folded hands over his paunch and lowered his head in concentration. "I've bad news for you, Chiresko. Word has reached me that you are wanted for questioning in connection with the rescue of Moriana."

"They'll never capture me! I'll die before I surrender!" Sweat streamed down the thin face.

"One hopes that will be unnecessary. Still, it would be best for you to remain unseen for a time. Possibly even to go to ground until the situation eases."

Agony etched Chiresko's face at the prospect of exile to the surface. Uriath turned to the table and ruffled through a sheaf of documents before saying, "I've arranged a temporary hiding spot for you, Chiresko. It is in the warehouse of Councillor Elura, near the starboard cargo docks."

For the third time in a week the residents of the City in the Sky thronged its narrow streets for a royal spectacle. The first had been the funeral procession of Queen Derora, culminating with her skull being placed in the pavement of the Skullway among those of other past rulers of the City. Next had been the Rite of Dark Assumption, unperformed for five millennia.

Now Synalon, elder daughter of Derora, was to be crowned queen.

Normally a coronation occasioned great joy. Men and women dressed in their finest clothes, apprentices raced and tumbled through the streets, wild with glee at having been freed from their chores for the day, and even the shaven-headed mages relaxed their professionally dour countenances into smiles. A coronation was a time of spectacle and merriment, a doing of bright magic, and feasting at the expense of the new monarch. Coronation Day was banners and bright streamers and the old songs of glory.

The weather seemed prepared to accommodate the usual spirit of the day. The sun shone, unhindered by clouds, and the rapid approach of winter slowed in defence to the occasion. The wind blew only enough to animate the pennons strung along the four broad thoroughfares of the City, emanating from the Circle of the Skywell.

The bands had turned out with their drums and flutes and widemouthed trumpets enameled in a thousand colorful designs. Behind them stood the massed ranks of the Sky City's soldiery.

First was a glittering like a forest of glass spires: the brightly burnished halberds of the Palace Guard. Next the City's infantry with shields, spears and conical helmets awaited the order for the procession to begin. Then the huge hounds of the Sky City cavalry, flown up by balloon from compounds on the surface, bayed at one another, avid to be freed from their riders' constraint. Last were the Monitors, sullen in the anonymity of their helmets. The whole parade coiled like a spring around the open area by the aft docks of the City into which the boulevard that followed the floating metropolis's long axis fed. Above it the City's bird-riders orbited in a carousel of wings, the drafts of their downbeats stirring the Palace Guardsmen's ornamental plumes. Higher still, the smaller circle of the Sky Guard's eagles slowly rotated.

Crowds framed the four great avenues, held back by

Monitors and infantry. Others jostled for position in the penthouses of the City's highest buildings. It was only a matter of time before an incautious spectator, like one of those who formed a living wreath around the spire of the Lyceum in the City's first quadrant, would fall to his death on the hard stone streets.

But though the onlookers crowded each other as vigorously as ever, a sullen stillness overlay the multitude. Anticipation touched the air, but it was not the restive, eager anticipation of some pleasurable event. It was the kind of anticipation that might greet the growth of a gigantic black cloud belched forth from the Throat of the Dark Ones, the volcano Omizantrim.

"Ah!" The City's populace sighed with one voice. The skyward-tumbling tracery of the Palace of the Skyborn dominated the horizon; its mighty central tower could be seen from any spot within the guardwall. From its apex a pair of wings unfolded, as black as a necromancer's robe.

The eagle took flight. Its fellows in the air above kept still the raucous cries of greeting or challenge with which one war bird customarily met another. Itself in silence, the jet-black bird flapped slowly around the perimeter of the City. On its back rode a slender figure, black hair streaming behind her.

The eagle circled the City once. Returning to the Palace, it flew past. It climbed in a spiral, passing the ring of common bird-riders, and boldly confronted the living crown that was the Sky Guard. A bird detached itself from the flock and flew to meet her. In appearance it was twin of the one the woman rode; the only difference was a fiery red crest on its head. Its rider was diminutive.

The rider of the crimson-crested bird voiced a challenge. Magic crystal set about the City caught his words and resonated them until it seemed the City itself spoke.

"Who dares intrude within the sky above our sacred City?"

"Your queen," came back the haughty reply. "By right of birth and justice."

"Then pass."

They turned back to join the circling Guard. The woman dropped her mount lower to be met by one from the ring of less exalted sky riders.

"Who dares spread wings among the towers of our blessed City?"

"Your queen, by acclamation of People and Council."

"Descend."

The watchers inhaled slowly as the black eagle wheeled down toward the waiting procession, wondering how the third ritual challenge would be answered. A soldier, by custom of the lowest rank, stood forth with halberd held horizontal to bar the way of the rider who grounded before him.

"Who dares set foot upon the streets of our most holy City?" he cried, his young voice shrill with emotion.

For five millennia of their rule, the Etuul had answered, *Your queen, by that peace my mothers brought you.* The raven-haired woman swung off her mount and placed herself in front of the Palace Guardsman.

"Your queen, by the favor of the Dark Ones who rule all!"

A shudder passed through the throng like ripples on a pond. For five thousand years those words had gone unuttered. What did they portend for those on whose ears they fell?

Tears gleamed on the young soldier's cheeks as he knelt in wordless acknowledgment.

Synalon turned. A Palace Guardsman took the reins of her eagle Nightwind and led the fierce giant to stand out of the way of the procession. Erect, taller than most of those over whom she placed herself this day, the princess strode toward the Circle of the Skywell.

With the parade following behind in a thumping of bootheels, clamor of trumpets and snap of banners in the rising breeze, Synalon came to the Circle, paced slowly around the yawning Well of Winds and walked on along the wide way to the forwardmost point of the City. There she knelt alone on the parapet, head bowed, speaking to herself the words of a secret incantation.

She rose, returning slowly to the procession. Musicians and soldiers broke ranks to let her through. Then they silently followed her back to the Circle.

There she turned left and paced to the starboard edge of the City. The process repeated itself, and soon she was back in the esplanade surrounding the Well. There she stood before the Council of Advisors, who sat upon bleachers carved from black onyx, and recited the oath of allegiance. To the ancient creed she appended the words, "I swear by the blood my mothers shed upon these stones to return the City to the greatness it once knew."

Face impassive, Uriath rose, took the winged silver crown from its pillow of state and walked to the princess. She fell to her knees before him. As Councillors Tromym and Elura draped the royal robe of black and purple feathers about Synalon's shoulders, Uriath rested the crown gently about her temples.

"All hail Synalon the First, Queen of the City and the Sky, Scion of the Skyborn, Mistress of the Clouds." He did not shout, but his voice rose as loud as all the trumpets.

The crowd's answering hail seemed less loud.

Synalon rose. Uriath fell to his knees and abased himself. The other councillors stood up from their seats and did the same. Under the watchful eyes of the Monitors the rest of the City's inhabitants dropped to one knee. The air quivered with the cries of eagles proclaiming the new queen.

Thus far she had deviated only slightly from custom. Now Synalon added an innovation of her own. She raised her arms above her head and voiced a high, discordant cry.

Like noisome spores from a bloated toadstool, ravens with talons dipped in dark poison burst from the eaves of the City in the Sky. Crying their own replies to their mistress's summons, they coalesced into a cloud of blackness above her head. The watchers reacted once more in unison—this time with loathing.

Synalon shed the simple slippers she wore. Barefoot, in deference to her ancestors, Synalon the Queen walked slowly over the skulls of the City's former rulers toward the open portals of her Palace.

Eagles fell from the sky like autumn leaves. Relieved of the awesome burden of ceremony, their riders called to each other across the rapidly filling Circle.

Herded by Monitors with lead-tipped staves, the Sky Citizens poured into the Circle. A banquet awaited them. But the quantity of food and drink weighting down tables set around the Well seemed less than suited to the majesty of the occasion. The festive mood of the throng, none too evident to begin with, faded further as the citizenry discovered the scant repast given them to celebrate the ascension of Synalon I.

Having shed solemnity along with his own feathered robe of ceremony, Uriath permitted himself a sardonic smile. He knew the reason for the niggardliness of the feast. Food and drink were expensive in the City since almost all had to be imported from the surface. The luxurious fare that usually accompanied a coronation cost a fabulous amount. Synalon did not intend to spend such a sum. She was determined upon war, and that demanded austerity in all things of minor import.

Her warlike intentions were supposed to be secret, known only to her innermost circle of advisors. Uriath's smile broadened. Near the center of the web of intrigue spun about the Palace, Uriath prided himself on keeping well informed as to everything happening along its strands.

The jet-black eagle landed nearby with an ear-straining screech of talons on pavement. Uriath nodded politely and looked away, pretending to engage his fellows in conversation. Preoccupied with the hunt for the fugitive princess and her lover and impatient to be off, Rann nodded briskly and strode off toward the Palace.

A second bird, egg-grey with flecks of slate, touched down near the prince's mount, Terror. Its rider swung down and handed the reins to a lackey. He was about to follow Rann when Uriath stepped forward and touched his sleeve.

"Colonel Chalowin," the red-faced councillor said. "A word with you."

The colonel's left cheek twitched almost hard enough to close his eye. "What is it?" he snapped. He had no time for courtesies, even to a high councillor.

Uriath studiously ignored the affront. Chalowin was a strange man, tall for a Sky Citizen and agonizingly thin. His brow high beneath dark hair and his cheekbones wide flanges, he looked more like a Josselit monk than one of the Skyborn. He was the sort of man to hurl himself at a problem and wrestle it down; in conversation his manner was that of an aggressor.

Except when the speaker was Rann. Then Chalowin settled into a curious calm, gazing at his commander with the mixture of fear and adoration common to all bird-riders. Chalowin worshiped the prince like an acolyte paying homage to his god.

Devoted as he was, the acolyte was less deadly perspicacious than his master. Uriath moistened his lips, made a conspiratorial sideways flick of his eyes and leaned closer.

"The queen and I have had our differences, Colonel," he said, "but I cannot countenance treason. Or traitors. There, I have something to tell you."

Chalowin cocked his head. His left eyelid fluttered like the banners that bedecked the City. His fingertips drummed on the lacquered scabbard encasing his sword.

Uriath brought his lips near the other's ear. He smelled the rankness of his breath. Uriath repressed a shudder, thinking how much this man seemed like a hunting bird, even to the stench.

"A plotter?" hissed Chalowin.

Uriath nodded. "Perhaps one privy to the nefarious scheme that allowed the criminal Moriana to escape her due punishment."

"Where?"

Uriath whispered briefly. Chalowin's head jerked back. His eye was almost shut. His left nostril pulsated in time with the tic. He shook himself and stalked off toward the Palace with no further word to Uriath.

"What was that about?" a voice called out.

Uriath suppressed a panicky start. He turned, his heart as spastic as the muscle in Chalowin's check.

"Nothing, my dear Tromym," he said. He accepted the vessel of golden wine his friend offered him. He squinted at the pewter mug cynically, then raised it. "A toast, good Tromym."

"What to, Uriath?"

The high councillor only smiled.

* * *

"Great Ultimate!" shrieked the girl with the short blond hair. "They've found us!"

Three men looked up from their game of draughts just as the door crashed inward in a cloud of splinters. A man stepped into the cavernous warehouse, his movements as sharp and sporadic as a lizard's. He wore tunic and trousers of purple and black.

"Him," he said, pointing with the naked blade in his hand. "Take him alive. The rest don't matter."

The girl lunged at him with a heavy knife. His scimitar turned it with contemptuous ease. Steel whispered. The girl looked down in surprise and disbelief at the stream of blood hosing from her throat.

"Shishol!" shrieked one of the youths as she sank lifeless to the sawdust-powdered floor. He charged, hands outstretched like claws, to impale himself on the javelins of the men who stepped in behind the swordsman.

The other conspirators bolted. They dodged for the rear of the warehouse, scrambling in and out among elephantine bales of cloth. The plumper one staggered and fell against a bale. He yipped with fear as a flung javelin grazed his calf. Then he recovered and dashed after his black-haired friend.

The emaciated black-haired youth burst out into an alleyway. To his left rose the four-foot guardwall marking the boundary of the City. Twenty yards in the other direction lay a street swarming with black-and-purple-clad soldiers.

He raced away from them, intent on reaching the short wall. His companion hesitated, uncertain of his friend's intent. A broadheaded arrow nailed him to the door. He died with the shadow of wings across his face.

Chiresko heard the hollow boom of wings stop as the Sky Guardsman dropped into the narrow space between warehouses. The confines of the alley left no room for the bird to flap its wings. With a leap Chiresko gained the top of the guardwall. Tottering on the brink of emptiness, he slumped against the corner of Elura's building.

The eagle shot by him like a living missile, claws stretched to clutch his torso. The bird missed by scant inches and plunged over the wall, its angry cries filling the narrow alley with hideous echoes.

Shouts sounded up the street. Time moved like molasses for him. He saw his pursuers spill into the alley. He saw his friend's dead body sagging against the door, head slumped to the side. He saw his own death approach.

Wings pounded air. The war eagle had recovered from its dive and returned intent on vengeance. As it neared Chiresko, its rider banked in toward the City's wall and grabbed at the black-haired rebel.

To his astonishment the boy leaped gladly to meet him. The bird-rider shouted hoarsely as Chiresko wrapped mad-strong arms about his neck.

A riderless eagle spun skyward, crying like an orphaned child. When the other Guardsmen reached the wall, all that remained was the wisp of Chiresko's laugh, stretching thin into the distance below.

CHAPTER
TWO

A small fire crackled fitfully inside the circle of rocks. The sere, scrubby grasses that grew in the shadow of the Ramparts burned smokelessly, so Fost pronounced it safe to build a fire. Fost took great care in making sure no stray spark would set ablaze the surrounding dry vegetation.

A haunch of meat sizzled over the flames. Having spent much of his life on the treeless steppe, Fost carried in his knapsack an iron spit and forked uprights for roasting game. After weeks of tasteless gruel and the stewed weeds of the Ethereals, the smell of cooking antelope produced a hunger in Moriana and Fost that was almost agony. The beast had broken from between two boulders in front of the travelers, a tiny yellow-and-cream buck with a flat, saw-edged horn growing from its snout. Useless for lack of arrows, Moriana's bow had long since been abandoned. But the antelope had popped up close enough for a well-aimed cast of the long knife Fost had given Moriana.

The pair had emerged from the Crater the previous afternoon to discover a landscape totally innocent of snow. The same capriciousness of climate that had brought an early blizzard howling through the Ramparts to threaten them a week ago had sent warm winds from the North to sweep away the snow. A chill still edged the air but it was bearable.

Fost lay full length on the ground, fingers interlaced behind his neck. Half-lidded eyes watched round clouds tumble by idly, but he didn't neglect to scan the horizon now and again for the sweep of great wings.

"If we didn't have Rann breathing down our necks," he said, "I'd find this the sheerest pleasure."

"I'm glad your bucolic tastes are so amply gratified," said Erimenes sourly.

Moriana looked at the courier with curiosity. "You like the cold and wind and harshness? Strange. I'd thought you city-bred."

"City-bred and -born," Fost said, laughing. "I first saw the day in the Teeming of High Medurim. A soot-faced, starving urchin of the streets, never resting, trusting no one, never sleeping twice in the same spot."

"You don't make it sound attractive. I'd always heard great things of the Imperial capital."

"Oh, Medurim's a city of wonder where every fantasy can be fulfilled—if you've the money. I never did. Born poor, die poor—that's the law the city lives by." He rolled to one side and prodded the roasting meat with the tip of his dagger to turn it. "Still, I miss it—in a way. For all its corruption it has a certain decayed grandeur like a noted courtesan grown old. It's still a melting pot for the Sundered Realm, and the port attracts merchantmen from all over the world. Caravels from the Isles of the Sun, barkentines from the Northern Continent, vessels from the Antipodes and the lands beyond the Golden Seas, all come to Medurim. I used to go down and sit by the docks and watch them come in. When I grew older I'd get work unloading them. Sometimes they'd pay me, other times they'd beat me and chase me off." He laughed. "Those who treated me shoddily came to regret it. I'd sneak back in the night and steal the choicest item from their cargoes. Ah, Medurim, a lovely, pox-ridden, treacherous bitch of a city. How I longed to be free of her!"

"You were a slave?"

"Only to my belly." He poked at the fire. "I was an apprentice for a time. An apprentice thief. Old Fimster was my master and he treated me well enough, beating me only when I deserved it. He raised me from an orphan pup; my parents were killed in a dole riot."

Moriana sat with her legs drawn up, arms clasped about her knees, chewing ruminatively on her lower lip. A flock of large shapes winged across the sky. Fost tensed only briefly. It seemed that forever wings in the sky had been a sign of mortal peril. He was as yet unaccustomed to the notion that sometimes they were signs of safety. No lone eagle would chance upon them while the thulyakhashawin hunted.

"The life history of a guttersnipe," the princess said, her words gently scoffing. "Surely there's more to it than that. You've come by education somehow. How'd you do it?"

"I stole it."

Moriana stared at him.

"Truly," Fost said. "I don't joke about such things. The library of Medurim is as big as a palace. It was once as glorious, but by my time had fallen into disrepair, with soot streaking the marble façades and many arcades collapsed with no attempt at restoration. The place always fascinated me. My friends derided the notion, but I was convinced that some fabulous treasure lay behind that vast columned portal."

He drew himself into a sitting position, eyes fixed on the leaping, sallow flames. "I slipped in one afternoon, intending to find that treasure and steal it. But I didn't find any treasure. Just books, shelves and shelves of books, so high a man needed a tall ladder to reach the topmost." He shook his head. "I stayed. I still don't know why. I wandered through the dusty shelves, pulling out books at random, opening them and scanning pages without comprehension. It frustrated me not understanding what those volumes contained. It seemed unfair. I tried by dint of effort to pry meaning from the pages. It didn't work.

"The hours passed. I fell asleep unnoticed in some dim recess of the library. In the morning I was shaken awake by a rheumy-eyed oldster wearing the indigo gown of a pedant. It scared me at first. He could have turned me in, you know, and I'd have been enslaved for vagrancy. He asked what I was doing there. Rather foolishly I told him. 'I thought there was treasure inside this great building, sire,' I said. 'I came to steal it.' "

Erimenes was making ostentatious sounds of yawning. Fost, knowing full well that the spirit had no need to yawn and only did so to make plain his boredom with the tale, continued without interruption.

"He laughed at this, the old man did. 'Well, treasure lies herein,' he said, 'but not anyone may partake of it.' And he took me on as his pupil, taught me to read and reckon and think thoughts beyond the gutter and my next meal."

"But how did you steal your education?" asked Moriana.

"Ceratith made his living as a tutor, though a meager living it was, for interest in learning had declined among the monied classes of Medurim. I couldn't pay, of course. Ceratith forever joked that I was robbing him." Fost's expression darkened. "It wasn't true. I always meant to pay him, if ever I could get together the money."

"Why didn't you?"

"I never had the chance. One night, as he wended his way home from the library, a pair of alley-bashers knocked in his skull. All he had on him was a devalued Old Empire klenor and three sipans." Fost rubbed his jaw. "A poor bargain for the thieves because I found them and killed them. Not long after that, Fimster died of an ague. I signed on with a collier bearing coal to North Keep to feed the hunchbacks' forges. I was fourteen at the time. That palled eventually, and when I turned seventeen I was working as a courier out of Tolviroth Acerte, the City of Bankers." He turned and slapped the satchel. "And that concludes the story of my life, friend Erimenes, so you can cease your show of tedium."

"No show," Erimenes said. "My ennui is perfectly genuine. But why stop now, just as you reach the most interesting parts: the fleshpots of Tolviroth."

"What do you know of fleshpots, Erimenes?" the courier asked.

"Not as much as I'd like to," admitted Erimenes. "That bothersome slug Gabric had no sense of adventure. He stuck me on a shelf and left me to rot until you arrived to take me to Kest-i-Mond."

"Gabric is a slug," Fost said. He chuckled. "He'll flay me alive for failing to report back, if ever I return to Tolviroth Acerte. I doubt I shall. The less time I spend in cities, the happier I am."

"Faugh," Erimenes said. "You're little better than Gabric. To show what a dolt your friend Fost's employer is, Moriana, my morsel, on one occasion a wench lissome and most comely pleaded with him not to foreclose on her. She had breasts like suva melons, but that obese capon ignored the obvious and repossessed her house. I ask you! He had no use for one more insect-ridden hovel and infinite use for a nice, rollicking tumble. But no, he allowed his greed to overwhelm his lust. The pinhead. He probably doesn't even like boys."

"We couriers have it that he frottages himself with his moneybags," Fost said. He cocked his head at his companion. "Why the troubled look, Moriana?"

"This talk of cities," she said. "It makes me wonder how my own fares." She rose and knelt by Fost's pack. "Do you mind if I borrow the water cask?"

"You didn't ask the first time you took it." He raised his head as she colored. "No, I'm sorry. Go ahead, do with it what you will."

She took the ebony chalice from the satchel and removed its lid. Instantly the vessel filled with water. She set it on the ground, hunkered down and closed her eyes.

Her lips fluttered. An eerie wail came from her that made hairs rise at the nape of Fost's neck.

"Interesting, isn't it, knowing a sorceress?" Erimenes said conversationally. "She could turn you into a newt any time she wished."

"You always look on the bright side of things, don't you?" Fost looked on with a combination of apprehension and interest as Moriana extended her fingers over the chalice. The water turned opaque white. It began to swirl round and round, as though stirred by a spoon.

She opened her eyes. The liquid cleared. But it was plain water no longer. Instead it was like a window overlooking a scene two hundred miles distant.

"Look upon the City in the Sky," she said.

Crowds thronged the Circle of the Skywell. But this was no mere mob of citizens as had gathered to watch Moriana's sacrifice; these stood in orderly ranks, armored in leather enameled with bright designs, bearing shield, spear and short, curved sword. Others marched before them, clad in plate and chain. Fost recognized the sallets of the Monitors. Squadrons of war eagles wheeled across the sky.

Muttering to herself, Moriana gestured. The picture changed. It showed lines of captives being herded to dungeons and heavily armed Monitors moving from house to house, smashing in doors and dragging unfortunates out to join the miserable procession. Next the docks came into view. Balloons, gigantic bloated sausages many times the size of the round gasbag Fost had ridden to the City, rubbed their flanks against the ramparts like amorous whales as files of slaves unloaded their gondolas.

Moriana shook her head sadly. The image disappeared, leaving behind only a tiny ripple.

"Insurrection?" Fost asked, though the pictures hadn't much looked like it.

"No. Synalon arms the City for war, training fresh troops, crushing all opposition, storing up provisions." She smoothed her hair back from her face. Sweat stood on her forehead despite the cool air. "She's confident, damn her. She no longer bothers to block my scrying spell."

"Who could threaten the City in the Sky?" Erimenes asked.

"None. Only the Fallen People might dare but they are few and lack the matériel." Fost raised his eyebrows at this, and made a note to ask her more about the descendants of the City's builders. Luranni's tales had piqued his curiosity. "No, my sister prepares for a war of conquest." She clenched her hands into knots of anger. "She will destroy all the Etuul have built. I must return. I must stop her!"

Fost did not answer. After a moment Moriana glanced at him and looked away. She'd trodden forbidden ground. The issue of who should have the Amulet of Living Flame and what should be done with it once they reached Athalau lay between them like a curtain of ice. By common consent they had avoided it until now.

Mercifully Erimenes broke the silence. "I'm forced to observe that this is an extravagant waste of a lovely afternoon. And pleasure, once wasted, can never be regained, and who knows better than I? Why don't you engage in a little copulation before the cold returns?"

Fost laughed too loudly. "Not a bad idea, if there

were more time. I've another idea." He grasped the ceramic handle of the skewer and raised the antelope leg. It was done to perfection. "Why don't we eat and restore our strength? We start into the mountains tomorrow."

"If you're wrong, rider, you know what to expect." Though softly spoken, the words carried clearly across the rush of wind and the rhythmic thunder of wings. The soldier so addressed urged his mount to greater speed.

Prince Rann was in a foul mood. His scouts had caught the fleeting princess and her accomplice within hours of their escape, only to have the fugitives best them in combat and vanish into the tangle of ravines north and west of Brev. The survivors admitted being afraid to press pursuit; they claimed their quarry had enchanted them. Nonsense, of course. Synalon's ward-spells protected them from adverse magics. But the damage was done, and the worst of all was that those responsible couldn't be punished for their cowardice and ineptitude. He had too few men to spend them in that fashion.

From the outset Rann assumed the fugitives would head southeast by the straightest route for the Gate of the Mountains. He'd acknowledged to himself the possibility they could have gone due south instead, to attempt passage through the Valley of Crushed Bones he'd seen marked on the map Synalon had found in the satchel with the spirit jar. Yet he'd had men sufficient only to scout one route and had opted for the one he thought more likely to be right. As a result he and his bird-riders spent two and a half weeks combing empty grassland without result. When they drew near the Ramparts, they ran the risk of encountering the winged foxes. Rann had lost four men to the beasts.

Next a storm blew out of the Cold Wastes beyond the mountains, taking the searchers by surprise and whirling five men to oblivion before the rest found the ground and safety. A man and two birds had frozen to death by the time the blizzard lifted and the sneering gods of chance sent a warm wind out of the North to scour off the new-fallen snow. The search had continued, as fruitlessly as before.

Then yesterday a rider scouting the patrol's back trail had been blown off course by high winds. His bird had seen something suspicious, which turned out to be disturbed earth above a dugout trench large enough to accommodate two people. It lay midway between the ravine country and the Great Crater Lake.

So now with his full strength Rann made for the lake to try to pick up the trail there. He had already promised himself that should this prove another false lead the rider who had reported the dugout would suffer, manpower shortage or not.

The multiple chevron formation of eagles knifed through the sky. Rann's eyes, scarcely less keen than those of his mount, scanned the land below for sign of the fugitives' passing. The bird he rode was not Terror, but a lighter, faster eagle, grey spotted with brown, that was more suited to reconnaissance work. The flight reached the Crater, hidden under its perpetual mound of steam. They made a slow orbit of the immense declivity, finding nothing. Rann's impatience mounted by the second.

At last Odol, the soldier who had reported finding the dugout, grew uneasy under the sidelong scrutiny of those tawny eyes.

"P—perhaps they were caught by the storm and sought shelter in the Crater's warmth. Their tracks wouldn't have outlived the melting of the snow, mi-lord."

Rann scowled at the man a moment longer, too distracted even to enjoy the other's obvious mental agony. Then, without a word, he banked his eagle and slipped into a spiral descending toward the cloud.

Shortly after, they broke through the clammy fog. Below them they saw a collection of dilapidated slag huts. Briefly Rann wondered what manner of primitives resided in such wretched dwellings. He steered his bird toward a cleared space roughly in the center of the village.

A crowd gaped in silent wonder as the bird-riders touched down before the large circular temple.

"There look to be fewer than a hundred souls living here," Rann said as he dismounted. "Captain Tays, take twenty men and round up the lot of them. Kill anyone who offers any resistance whatsoever." Tays, a swarthy, bandy-legged man even shorter than his prince, grinned, bobbed his head and trotted away, calling together a squad as he went.

Rann drew off his thick gauntlets. Scowling, he looked around. He'd taken the group of villagers standing about in the square to be women initially, but now he saw there were men among them in about equal numbers. The males of the town had a delicate, almost dainty look to them and their features looked little different from the women's. The bodies of both sexes were so willowy as to make it difficult to distinguish between them. Onlookers began turning away with an air of complete indifference.

The prince had known groundlings to react to the arrival of the eagle-riders of the Sky City with various emotions: fear, awe, dismay. He had never known the Guard to be greeted with indifference.

"You there," he said, striding toward the nearest villager. "I say, I'm talking to you. *Answer*." Neither word nor movement gave any sign that the man had heard. Flushing, Rann nodded to a soldier.

A javelin whistled through the air to smack between the villager's shoulder blades. He pitched forward onto his face and lay still. Not a sound had come from him.

Tays's party returned, herding a group of the tall, wispy folk with the points of spears and scimitars. The captain's blade was bloody, but he wore a puzzled expression.

"These are strange folk, my Prince," he called. "They don't fear death." He scowled at the several dozen captives his men had rounded up. "I think they just came along to humor us."

Rann's scowl etched itself deeper in his visage. He had an uncomfortable feeling that the captain had just experienced one of his rare glimmerings of insight.

"Then we'll have to teach them, won't we?" he said. "Slay ten of them, and we'll see how apt our pupils are."

He turned a smile toward the assembled villagers. Javelins stabbed, sword blades cleaved flesh. Dark blood stained the gowns of the doomed ten. They fell, yet no sound came from their lips as they died.

"They don't even moan," a bird-rider exclaimed.

Approaching another man, Rann fought the urge to draw his sword and hew him down. What was wrong with these people? Were they mad or imbeciles? With apparent civility he asked, "Who are you?"

"I am Gedrhus," he answered. "We are the Ethereals."

"I seek a blond woman and a large man with black hair. Have they been here?"

The Ethereal considered the matter. "I have seen many blond women and black-haired men. All of them were here, for I have been to no other place."

Snarling, Rann ripped free his sword and slashed open the man's stomach. "Insolent pig!" he snapped. "You think to make me the butt of your puny joke?"

The Ethereal dropped to his knees. "I don't understand," he said, his voice unchanged. "I feel you are too much of the material. Free yourself from the bonds of ill and . . ." Rann's scimitar split his head, finishing the sentence for him.

Rann snapped orders. Bird-riders hurried to obey them. Trees grew within the Crater. In a short time the soldiers had assembled a pile of wood, both raw lumber and the crude furniture they found in the slumping huts. Rann paced nervously back and forth, his blood singing in anticipation, as an Ethereal was stripped, bound to a pole and suspended above the pyre. At Rann's command the wood was lit.

The prince awaited the first groaning cry of agony as the flames commenced their dance. The Ethereal continued to gaze skyward as if nothing out of the ordinary was happening. His flesh reddened, blistered and began to slough off and blacken. Rann bounced up and down on the balls of his feet. The smell of roasting flesh tickled his nostrils. For once it failed to beguile him.

Flames cloaked the bound man. He made no response.

"What's wrong with you?" Rann shouted. "Cry, scream, plead, do something!" He went to his own knees beside the fire, so close the fur edging of his cloak began to smoulder. "Beg for release from your torment. No, not even that; ask and I shall set you free. But *speak!*"

The man's hair burned now, surrounding his face with a ghastly wreath of fire. He turned his head toward Rann, and the prince's heart rose as he saw emotion touch the mild brown eyes.

"You interrupted my dance," the Ethereal said. His head slumped as life fled him.

Almost weeping with frustration, Rann rose and turned away from the charring corpse. "Bring me another," he commanded. A woman was tied to a stake driven into the dirt of the square. Drawing a special knife he carried for such occasions, Rann went to work on her with all the consummate artistry of which he was capable. It had no more effect than the roasting of the man. Another captive followed her in a death that would have sent the bravest warrior raging into madness with pain. Another followed, and another. The victims sang or spoke of epistemology and teleology or simply stared, each oblivious to the abuse being wrought upon his or her body.

At last Rann slumped in a chair and regarded his prisoners. They stood before him, calm and contemplative, virtually ignoring him. His mind wrestled with the challenge of how to eke some response from these folk since physical torture had failed. Among his talents Rann numbered the ability to read infallibly the weaknesses of those with whom he came in contact, which made him an accomplished warrior as well as a sadist. A few moments' worth of hard thought produced a new line of attack.

"Hear me," he said in a deceptively mild voice. "I'm convinced that the woman Moriana and the man Fost have passed this way. Unless you tell me of them, when they arrived, how long they stayed and where they have gone, I shall cut off the feet of every person in this village. Next I shall cut off the hands. Then I will remove the ears, puncture the drums and pluck forth the eyes from their sockets. Finally, if no one has spoken the words I wish to hear, I shall tear your tongues from their roots and leave you here to die, helpless."

An uneasy murmur ran through the Ethereals. Rann smiled. He had gauged them right at last. His men, searching the village, had brought him word of the statuary, musical instruments and crystal phials of essence they discovered in abundance. These folk clearly devoted their lives to meditating upon what they held to be various forms of beauty. He thought they wouldn't like to be denied all contact with loveliness, for all their words about scorning the material world.

A man stepped forward. "I remember ones such as you describe."

A cry rose from the prisoners. An Ethereal lunged forward, his golden hair in disarray, his ocean-blue eyes wide.

"You mustn't tell them, Itenyim. We must hold true to our beliefs. We cannot betray—unnh!" The head of a javelin sprouted from the right side of his chest. Scarlet doused the front of his white robe.

"I am sorry, Selamyl," said Itenyim. "I cannot bear the thought of being denied my art." Selamyl's mouth worked in supplication, his hands reached forth. Blood gushed from his mouth as he fell.

"Well," said Rann, feeling at ease for the first time in a fortnight, "come and sit at my side and make yourself comfortable, good Itenyim. We have much to discuss, we two."

"The magic of Athalau," Erimenes said in his most resonant tones, "was, at least in later years, not so much magic per se. True sorcery involves the manipulation of powers external to oneself. Our so-called magic came from within our own minds. We schooled ourselves to seek out and cultivate our latent mental powers, using them exclusively to gain the ends of sorcery. Consequently common protective enchantments have little or no effect on Athalar magic."

The spectral figure folded blue, glowing hands over its middle. "Nonetheless, the city of Athalau itself possesses talismanic qualities in relation to our magic, largely by virtue of the place it occupied in many of the mental exercises we employed to discipline our minds."

"In other words," said Fost, trying to bite back a yawn, "the closer you get to Athalau, the stronger your powers become."

"Such a bald statement oversimplifies questions of the utmost philosophical complexity," the spirit said, "but essentially, yes."

Moriana gazed into the low fire. They had ascended far enough into the Ramparts to think it safe to light one at night. It was unlikely the Sky Guardsmen would chance the treacherous downdrafts of these mountains in the dark on their night-blind birds.

"So you were able to stimulate us when our bodies threatened to give out during the storm by working on our minds," she said.

"And able to keep me from revealing your continued existence to the Ethereals," Fost said, leaning against the sheer rock face along which they'd camped.

"But you rendered us invisible to the Guardsmen when we were many miles north of here," Moriana said. "What can you do this close to your home?"

"Don't build an exalted conception of my powers," Erimenes said. "Recall that I couldn't constantly maintain the illusion of your invisibility. My powers have grown, true, but they are far from infinite. Besides, most of the applications of my abilities, sad to say, lack any practical application in the present instance."

"Tell me, Erimenes," Fost said. The spirit turned toward him, a look of benign but thoroughly superior indulgence on his ascetic features. "Your powers stirred us to renewed exertion during the blizzard. Why couldn't they have roused us from the stupor of the Ethereals?"

Erimenes touched his nose with a fingertip. "I tried. The grip of those worthless creatures' drugs and spells, and your own desire to slip free of reality, held you too tightly for my mental skills to break you loose. You two had to free yourselves, though I was able to provide a suitable verbal stimulus."

Fost paced uneasily between the fire and the rock face. He paused and gazed up the narrow crevice that split the masses of the cliff. A long slope, steep but climbable, rose up to where black rock framed a wedge of stars. The instincts of a street urchin kept him from bedding down without having an escape route handy.

Worry nibbled at his mind. Erimenes's explanations were glib and plausible enough. Yet Fost had come to know the spirit well, too well to trust him very far. The whole matter of Erimenes's powers—and why he bent them to aid Fost and Moriana—raised far more questions than had been answered.

"Come, Erimenes, surely someone as wise as yourself has any number of useful skills," said Moriana. "What other miracles can you perform?"

Apparently unaware of the sarcasm in her voice, the scholar raised himself to his full height. He pondered for a moment, and his eyes opened wide.

"Just now," he said pompously, "I perceive a group of between twenty-five and forty men approaching furtively up the hill. You'd best act quickly. They're almost on top of us."

Moriana's jaw dropped. Cursing, Fost kicked out the fire. A shower of embers rained down the slope, illuminating the faces and forms of men. The courier reached down, scooped up Erimenes's jar and slammed the cap back into place.

"Take them!" a voice cried in the darkness. A spear bounced off stone with a jagged noise, striking sparks as it went. Fost jammed the jug into his satchel and tossed it to Moriana.

"Run," he told her. "Climb up the crack while I stand them off."

"I can't leave you," she said. Her sword hissed into her hand.

Dark forms reared all around. Fost parried a sword-cut purely by instinct and riposted, eliciting a cry of agony. Moriana crossed blades with a dimly seen antagonist and sent him rolling down the mountain, spewing blood from a punctured lung.

"Go, I tell you," Fost roared. "I can stand them off here awhile. Wait for me—use your judgment how long."

He turned to her. Their gazes briefly locked. Moriana nodded convulsively, spun and was gone, scrambling up the slope, leaving a wake of tumbling pebbles.

Fost heard the voice of Erimenes complaining aggrievedly at having to miss what promised to be an epic fight. Then the Sky Guardsmen charged.

CHAPTER THREE

erable pitch, but still Fost came on, swinging his blade until he waded knee-deep through slimy black foulness.

Then he was beside the pulsating fat body of the

Moriana stumbled and almost turned back as the sound of battle broke loose behind her. Grinding her jaw against the ache within, she made herself keep clambering up the shifting floor of the rock chute. Her lungs worked like bellows by the time she gained the top, and pain knifed through her ribs at every breath. But she was alive and safe—for the moment.

At the top she rested, panting. From below rose hoarse shouts, the clang of steel on steel, cries of pain as weapons found their mark. Hope glowed briefly in the princess. The fact that the din continued proved that her lover still held his own. Even as slightly built as they were, no more than two bird-riders could charge him at any time as long as he stayed within the mouth of the fissure. His greater strength and size would have a telling effect in such conditions.

Then a new thought staggered her. "Erimenes!" she hissed, shaking the satchel and climbing unsteadily to her feet. "We must go back. You can make Fost invisible and we can get away!"

"Restrain your emotions, my dear." His patronizing intonation enraged her, and she started to dash his jug against a jutting of rock. "Wait! It would do no good, as Fost realized, and as you would too, if you paused to consider."

Moriana slumped back to the loose rock. She saw what the spirit meant. Even if Erimenes could befuddle so many bird-riders at once, the fugitives would gain nothing by it. The wily Rann had cordoned them against the cliff before moving in. Even invisible, Fost and Moriana would have had no chance to slip past the attackers. If both had gone at once, with no one to secure the bottom of the crevice, the Sky Guardsmen could have stood below and volleyed arrows up the chute. With such a narrow arc of fire to cover, they couldn't have missed, whether or not their targets could be seen.

All this Fost had known at once and acted accordingly. Moriana reproached herself. She should have seen it too. Her fears for the Sky City were obsessing her, wearing down her mind. She could do nothing to help her people if through worrying she grew careless and was killed.

The ringing of swords no longer drifted up the chimney. Moriana's heart lurched. Had Fost fallen? She heard a rattling, scraping sound like metallic hail, and a voice raised in a bold shout of derision. There was no mistaking Fost's defiant cry. Rann had obviously ordered missile troops to the fore, and Fost had just as obviously weathered their first storm of projectiles.

She jumped up, knowing she shouldn't dawdle. Though to flee smacked of betrayal, she couldn't help the courier. *He gave his life to buy time,* Fost had said when grief for her fallen war bird had threatened to drag her down. *Let's not waste it.* If Fost somehow escaped Rann, she was confident he would catch up to her in time. If he fell . . . well, he wouldn't want his own death wasted either.

Settling the satchel's sling more comfortably over her shoulder, she set off. The twin moons had long since set, an event for which Rann had doubtless waited before ordering his assault. The rock underfoot tended to break beneath her weight and slip away. She fell constantly until her arms and knees were a mass of bruises.

"By the Great Ultimate," Erimenes complained when they had ascended a torturous five hundred feet, "must you keep bumping me about so? You're as clumsy as that leadfooted Fost."

Moriana dropped to a flat rock. A narrow trail

stretched behind, curving out of sight around the flank of the mountain. Beyond the path the land dropped away sharply. It was a miracle that one of her many stumblings hadn't carried her over the rim.

She wiped sweat from her forehead, felt a stickiness and held her hand close to her eyes to examine it. Her lacerated palm bled freely. She'd just smeared blood across her face.

"If you don't like traveling with me, I can drop you down a crevice somewhere, so you can enjoy peace and solitude for another fourteen hundred years," she told the spirit.

"Thirteen hundred and ninety-nine," Erimenes corrected mechanically. "You will do no such thing. You need the amulet too badly, if ever you're to have hope of defeating your sister. And you need me to find the amulet."

Moriana nodded wearily. She couldn't deny the truth of what he said. Freeing the City from Synalon's oppression was worth any sacrifice, even enduring Erimenes's endless prattle.

What troubled her was what the spirit needed her for. She had seen ample evidence of the late sage's capacity for treachery. The shade was utterly without loyalty. Yet he had interceded time and again in the last few weeks to save her and Fost from recapture by Rann. *Why?* she asked herself. *Back in the City he seemed to find Synalon and Rann more to his taste than us.*

I know why I need him. But why does he need me?

She sighed and pushed herself erect. She would learn the answer eventually, though she had a premonition she wouldn't care for it very much. Right now the only thing to do was climb.

False dawn had begun lightening the sky when she reached the meadow. The warm north winds had melted the snow. Grass grew green and lush and soft. A streambed, drying now that the runoff was gone, provided Moriana an upward route. The bed rose in a brief cliff, its rock worn smooth by running water. Climbing the dead waterfall took the last of Moriana's strength. At the top she threw herself down on the grass, drinking in icy air in gasps, the grass-smell rich in her nostrils with the lying promise of spring.

"You mustn't tarry like this," Erimenes chided her.

"Just let me rest a minute."

"If I do, you might not escape the bird I sense approaching."

"Bird?" She rolled onto her back, her sword hissing into her hand. *Has Rann sent men on birds after me, despite the darkness?* She scanned the sky intently. No vast cruciform shapes occluded the southern constellations. "I see nothing," she said. "Erimenes, if you're . . ."

A shadow loomed above her. Instinctively she rolled and felt something graze her shoulder. She continued her roll, coming to her feet in a crouch, the scimitar tasting the air in front of her.

A bird stood before her in the darkness but a bird unlike any she'd ever seen before. At least as tall as a Sky City eagle, it lacked a war bird's grace of form and movement. Ungainly, it waddled toward her, swaying on thick legs, powerful clawed toes gripping the ground. It stirred its wings restlessly, a sign only of agitation. The foot-long stumps were plainly vestigial and incapable of raising its considerable weight.

The knobby head slowly swiveled. It lacked eyes. Instead a single strip stretched across its head above the blunt, massive beak, dark but gleaming in the starlight like an insect's carapace. The head turned toward her, then stopped. The bird advanced.

"But it's got no eyes," she gasped, retreating slowly. "How can it see me?"

"It doesn't see you, obviously," Erimenes said. "It does, however, perceive the heat of your delectable body with some keenness, particularly in this chill." He made a speculative sound. "We knew them in my day, of course, but they didn't grow this large then. I wonder if they've changed in other ways."

Glancing over her shoulder, Moriana backed away. She had to be certain she didn't trip over a rock. If she fell, she had no doubt the monster would be on her in an instant, striking with its heavy beak. This time the beak would do more than simply glance off her shoulder.

The bird made no move to attack as Moriana slowly gave ground.

"It's curious," Erimenes explained. "It's never encountered anything like you before and wonders what manner of creature it's about to make a meal of."

She licked her lips. The legs were long, at least half its height. If she bolted, it would overtake her within five yards. The stony wall of the valley lay twice that distance behind her.

If it just stays curious a few breaths longer . . .

As she turned her head to check the path, the monster charged.

The rustle of talons on grass gave her a heartbeat's warning. She threw herself back and to the side, lashing out blindly with her sword. The blade clattered against hardness, slipped and then bit briefly. At the same instant, agony raked across her ribs. She scrambled away on all fours, panting with the pain in her side.

The bird lifted its hideous, naked head and loosed a squall of rage. Moriana's scimitar had struck its beak and had been deflected down to lay open its shoulder. Blood flew from the tip of its wing as it shook the stumpy limb in wrath.

I've only made it mad, she thought. *My next cut must tell, if it's not to finish me. Gods, it's big!*

Moriana's blood shone on the talons of its left foot. The monster had kicked out, trying to eviscerate her. Moriana drew her long knife and moved to meet the sightless hunter.

Hissing savagely, it attacked with beak and talons simultaneously. The knife blocked the beak, but the axelike blow sent the weapon spinning from Moriana's grip. Her scimitar bit deep into the striking leg, chopping through the bone. With an anguished wail, the bird collapsed.

Moriana ended its life with a sword-cut, dancing back barely in time to escape the final lunge of its beak. Shaking, she went to retrieve her knife.

"A monster, that one," she said, wiping slimy blood from her blade with a handful of grass.

"Don't grow complacent," Erimenes said. "You handled yourself bravely and skillfully. I've no complaints about the quality of the fight. On the other hand you do have a problem."

"What's that?" the princess asked, sliding her sword back into the improvised belt.

"What do you plan to do about the rest of the pack?"

In their eagerness to be first to get at the courier, the Sky Guardsmen completely forgot their discipline and training. Fost retreated into the crack. Three bird-riders lunged in after him, only to find themselves crowded too tightly together to use their weapons to full effect. Fost's broadsword licked out. The Guardsmen fell. Only one showed sign of life, and that was a feeble groaning.

"Do you want more?" Fost asked them, exultant at this initial victory. He didn't fail to heed the small voice in his skull that reminded him how many more bird-riders the night held. But a wild, fatalistic exhilaration settled on him as his dream of immortality evaporated. It was as though a burden dropped from his shoulders. He had lost all fear; the fight was all that mattered.

I almost wish Erimenes was here to see it, he thought.

He was not so giddy that he missed the curt order, "Back! Give the archers a shot, you groundborn scum!"

Man-high rocks flanked the entrance of the fissure. With a bound, Fost was behind one. An arrow skimmed his calf, ripping the rough breeches he'd put on after leaving the Ethereals' village. Other missiles bounced from the rocks with an iron clamor. His boulder shielded him completely.

He had his dagger in hand as well as the basket-hilted broadsword. A javelin probed around the rock sheltering him. The dagger slammed against its haft, pinning it to the stone, while Fost stabbed around the obstruction. The bird-rider gasped and carried the sword groundward as he fell. Fost yanked the blade free, roaring in triumph.

Darts and arrows winged up the crack. Close behind the volley came another rush of the Guardsmen. Fost slashed open the chest of the first to cross his vision and leaped out to confront the rest, hacking and thrusting with his broadsword, parrying with the dagger. A scimitar cracked against his hilt, a blow that would have halved his hand but for the protecting steel backet. His riposte went through the soldier's throat.

"Come on," he shouted at them. "You're no more men than he who leads you!"

Dead silence stretched down the rocky slope. Torches had been lit to illuminate the mouth of the fissure. Fost watched goblin shadows dance on the stony walls.

"Stand back," he heard a calm voice say.

Cautiously Fost peered around the side of his boulder, ready to jerk back out of an arrow's path. "Come and die, half-man," he cried, spitting on the ground before him.

Rann's face turned the color of sunbleached bone. "You won't have the lingering death you deserve," he said, his words still flowing like liquid amber, "because you force me to come up there and kill you now." His scimitar lightly gripped in a gloved left hand, he started up the slope.

Awaiting him, Fost held himself poised, alert for treachery. He had no doubt Rann would face him alone; any man who would put himself between the Vicar of Istu and the object of its wrath, armed only with a puny sword, possessed courage to match the prince's cruelty. Besides, his life lay on it. The longer Fost held the gap, the more likely Moriana was to escape. A point would come when Synalon would no longer accept failure, even on the part of her cousin, the prince. But Rann specialized in lethal cunning. Fost would take nothing he did at face value.

At the mouth of the crevice Rann threw himself face first on the ground. Three archers stood behind him, weapons nocked. Instantly they let fly at the courier's broad chest.

He was no longer there. The arrows passed harmlessly on to shatter against the rock wall. Rann's first unusual motion had sent Fost jumping back. Rann bounced up now, his left arm a blur of motion.

Springing up to pounce on his presumably disabled foe, Rann was just in time to catch Fost's dagger inside the joint of his right shoulder.

Rann sagged back. His smile went sickly. Reaching up with his sword hand, he extended two fingers and a thumb from his hilt and plucked the blade from the wound with no further change of expression. Casually he tossed the knife aside.

"Let's end this farce," he said.

Their blades crossed in a geometry of line and curve. Barely turning a low-line thrust with a twist of his wrist, Fost felt his berserker fever dissolve. A normal man would have been handicapped by the flowing wound in his shoulder, to say nothing of a man who still nursed ribs cracked by a demon's hand. Yet Rann's sword hand moved with sure precision, and his feet made no misstep. His foe would need both skill and luck to walk away from this encounter.

Far from disabling his opponent, his dagger cast had served solely to deprive Fost of his parrying weapon. He felt its need sorely now, with Rann's scimitar insinuating itself past his every defense to lick like a steel tongue at his flesh. The sword's caresses were light still, but each touch spilled more of the big man's blood and weakened him that much further. Nor would his strength serve to best the prince. Fost tried a widely swung powerhouse blow, and in turn received a cut across his belly that made him blink with pain. Had the scimitar bitten the breadth of a finger deeper his guts would have fallen around his knees in loops.

Rann did not go unscathed. A whistling stroke nicked an ear and a sudden lunge drew a bloody line along the side of his neck. But it was obvious the big man was wearing down more rapidly.

The decision came abruptly. Fost blocked a sidewise cut at his middle, only to have Rann turn his wrist unexpectedly. The tip of the scimitar whipped down and sank in the great muscle of Fost's right thigh.

Fost reeled back, hoping desperately the blade hadn't severed the main artery. If it had, he would be dead as soon as the shock wore off and the artery opened. But that could be a blessing; the leg gave way beneath him and he sat down with his back to the wall of the fissure. His resistance was at an end.

Rann whipped his sword through a blood-streaked arabesque and brought the hilt to his lips in a mocking salute.

"I hail you, courier. You've given me a better fight than I've enjoyed in years." He smiled wickedly. "Also, I perceive my men can now overpower you. It appears we'll come to know each other better, you and I."

Fost never knew afterward what moved him to speak the words, whether fear or desperation or something else had made his mind fall back on half-held faith. Fending off the prince with his sword, Fost raised his head and shouted, "I call upon my patrons, Gormanka of the Couriers and Ust, Red Bear of the East, to aid me now against these devil worshipers."

The response was all he could have asked for. At once an eerie wailing rose into the night from somewhere down the mountainside. Rann turned, as mystified as Fost, who sat with one hand pressed to his thigh and the other holding his broadsword aimed at the prince.

Again the cry, shrill and despairing. Consternation showed on the soldiers' faces. It was the sound of war birds, not only in pain but in fear—a sound no living ear had ever heard.

A torchbearer flew into the air, snatched up by something that rose behind him as though growing from the rocks themselves. His torch limned a snarling visage, immense jaws opened wide and a furry head with flattened ears and flame-dancing eyes advanced. The jaws clamped shut with a crunching sound. The torch fell.

More huge, misshapen figures loomed out of the blackness. Demons rode them, striking out with long spears and clubs. Grunting and whuffling, their mounts shuffled forward, titanic bears whose paws scattered bird-riders like straw dolls.

Rann ran at them, shouting orders. Arrows and javelins flew; a bear reared screaming and dropped, crushing its rider against a knife-edged outcropping. The bear-riders charged up the slope, led by a giant who swung a six-foot sword in fiery arcs.

The lead bear came among the score of Sky Guardsmen who'd followed Rann's commands. Sword and talons struck, men died. The Sky Guardsmen broke. Running as fleetly as any among them went Rann. It was one thing to interpose himself between his cousin and an animated statue gone amok; it was quite another to face an army of monster-riding fiends who'd swept out of nowhere to take his men in the rear and butcher them as blithely as they themselves had massacred Ethereals. The old campaigner in him took over, and with the demoralized remnants of his troops, he disappeared beyond the boundary of torchlight.

The bear paused for a moment to allow its rider to hurl imprecations after the fleeing Guards. Then it turned and lumbered toward Fost. The courier had just about come to the conclusion that his mind had snapped.

A whiff reached his nostrils, laden with the searing, musky tang of bear. He screwed his face up.

"Ust, what a stench!"

"You're very welcome," the bear-rider boomed. "We save you from certain death at the hands of the Sky people, and you thank us with insults. Truly you northern folk have odd notions of courtesy."

Fost shook his head. "I'm sorry. I'm not at my best just now. Besides, I didn't think you were real."

The giant swung off the bear's back and stepped forward. To Fost's astonishment his benefactor was a woman as tall as he and a little lighter, her bare arms bulging with muscle that rippled as she stirred. A tightly-laced leather bodice restrained breasts of surpassing fullness. Over it was thrown a fur vest and a

gorget of mail. Black breeches lined inside the thigh
with leather and knee-high boots completed her outfit.
Though far from beautiful, her face was strikingly
handsome, eyes blazing blue from a tanned, high-cheek-
boned face beneath an upright shock of hair the color
of flame.

A smile split the face. "Ask the bird-lovers how real
we are." She looked off in the direction the Guards had
taken. "Run, you cowards! Run or we'll catch you and
take your scrotums for medicine bags!"

"A bit late for that, in Rann's case," Fost murmured.
"My name is Fost, and I am in your debt for saving my
life."

"Jennas," she acknowledged, her head dipping curtly.
"You owe me nothing." She knelt and pried Fost's
fingers from his wound. He winced as her fingers
probed. "I confess we tarried overlong in coming to
your rescue. We came upon the Sky folk unseen and so
witnessed your stand. Well and bravely fought, if stupidly. You should never have let yourself be trapped
so."

She rose and took a roll of linen bandages from a
pack fixed to the bear's harness. The beast stood plac-
idly, peering at Fost. Blood dried blackly on its muzzle.

Skillfully Jennas began to bandage his wound. "We
get few strangers in this land. The Sky folk we know,
and their name has a foul taste in our mouths. Most
others have been spies for those who seek to subdue us.
So, as a general rule, we kill all who are unknown to
us." She tested the binding for tightness, nodding in
satisfaction at her handiwork.

"Why did you help me?" Fost asked.

"Stupid," she repeated. "Or in shock. Do you truly
not know?" He shook his head. "You called for aid
upon the Sun Bear. We are his people, the People of
Ust."

CHAPTER FOUR

"Perhaps 'pack' isn't the proper word," Erimenes said as Moriana sprinted into the litter of large rocks covering the valley's slope. Squawking stridently, the file of dark shapes that had been slowly stalking toward her up the valley broke into a long-legged run. "It may be that 'flock' is the correct collective, considering that these beasts, after all, are avian in nature."

"Why didn't you tell me that they hunted in groups?" Moriana gasped, choking down a groan as she slammed her knee against a stone. Behind her the blind birds, attracted by the heat ebbing from its body, had found their fallen comrade. They set up a shrill keening that flayed Moriana's nerves.

"Why, I was unsure until I sensed the bulk of them stealing up on you," the philosopher said. "As I stated before, they have changed in form since my mortal years; I didn't know whether their habits had varied as well. I presume now that they have not."

"Marvelous." Crouching behind a boulder, Moriana peered into the meadow. An indeterminate number of the giant birds clustered about the corpse, their heads swiveling on their hairy-feathered necks. One's eyeless face fixed on the princess. Instantly it uttered a shriek and ran straight at her.

"How many are there?" she asked, turning and scrambling up the slope.

"In the olden days they seldom numbered more than a hundred to a pack, if you will stipulate for the moment that it is a suitable term." Moriana made a noise of exasperation that Erimenes chose to interpret as assent. "I never knew of a group fewer than twenty. Of course, their numbers may have dwindled as their individual size increased, since it takes more food to support each one." The shade paused, apparently undisturbed by the jostling of his pack as the princess fled over and around the boulders strewn across the incline. "One thing appears unchanged. They are intensely social animals and will pursue to the end of their endurance anyone who has slain one of their number."

Moriana slumped against a leaning menhir, her strength exhausted. The sounds of the chase drew nearer. Realizing that the long legs of the birds made them far faster than she over open ground, she had headed instinctively for the cover of the rocks. But even here the birds held an advantage. Their big claws could grip protrusions and irregularities in the stone better than her hands and feet.

"Observe," Erimenes began. Moriana silenced him with a swat of her hand to his satchel.

"Be quiet," she whispered. "They'll hear you."

"Oh, rubbish," said Erimenes loudly. "They know perfectly well where you are. They can sense the heat of your body rising from behind this wretched rock, and your breath displays your presence like a column of smoke."

Moriana just had time to digest this intelligence when a bird came scuttling over the top of her boulder. Warned by the scratch of claw on stone, she danced back and threw up her blade to ward off a whirlwind assault of talon and beak. Somehow she blocked the blows with half-instinctive turns of her wrist, the beak clanging from metal like blows of a hammer. The scimitar licked in above reaching claws and the monster went down, gurgling blood from a gash in its throat.

Moriana darted away as a wave of birds broke over her rock. For a time they nattered in confusion. But shortly they caught her heat-signature again and the chase was on. Sightless, the hunters possessed a lethal edge over their quarry. In the dark her eyes were all but useless, while their heat-sense told them her exact location.

There must be a way to mask my heat, she thought. An idea came to her. "Erimenes," she panted. "Find me some vegetation, quick—the drier the better."

"That won't hide you any better than the boulders."

"Do it!"

With ill grace, the sage's ghost directed the princess to a stand of stunted cedars high up near the crest of the ridge that flanked the grassy valley. Some blight had killed them, yet they stood, bent and twisted like emaciated dwarves. Their limbs snapped with dry cracks as she bore down on them.

A burst of energy born of sheer panic had carried Moriana well in advance of her monstrous pursuers. But their cries rose behind her like the baying of hounds, coming inexorably closer with each passing second. Her lips moved in a half-remembered spell. She'd never been the sorceress her sister was, particularly in this complex and exquisitely perilous branch of the art.

For a heart-stilling instant nothing happened. The birds screamed triumphantly as they burst from the rocks and bore down upon the lifeless grove, their claws kicking up a shower of pebbles. Desperate, Moriana shrieked the final words of the invocation.

A sun blossomed within her. She cried out as intolerable heat traveled up her body to her shoulder and down her arm, casting a lurid white glow as though her flesh itself had become incandescent. The blazing agony reached her fingers, and a fire elemental burst from their tips and shot like a fireball into the scrub.

The desiccated wood took fire at once. Flames leaped high with a popping whoosh and the burbling laughter of the salamander chilled her soul. Rank, cloying smoke clutched at Moriana's throat. Coughing, she staggered out of the young inferno her magic had caused.

The birds went mad. The blaze of flame was like a blinding light flashed into a human's eyes in the dead of night. The creatures never had encountered fire before, particularly not the supernatural heat of the elemental. In their astonishment some of the huge killers flung themselves into the conflagration. Their cries rose in a horrid crescendo as the sprite devoured their flesh.

Weakened by the effort of conjuration, Moriana staggered away. With no fire to draw the salamander, the only heat available was that of Moriana's own body; the possibility had existed that the salamander would remain within her as it attained fiery life and consume her own flesh before breaking free. She had rid herself of the being in time but she had no idea how much harm it might have done her. She could barely manage the power to put one foot in front of the other, but that didn't matter now. The burning grove totally obscured her own bodily heat. The blind predators had no way to follow her.

A hundred yards away she stopped and performed the dismissal. The salamander resisted but was finally forced back to where it had come from. Its final shriek of rage stretched across the night like a banner. Though weariness tried to cement her limbs to the bench of stone where she paused, she drove herself to her feet and onward through the darkness.

When she had left the valley of the sightless birds by climbing another nearly dry waterfall, which Erimenes assured her rose too steeply for the hunters to scale, she dropped to the grass and slept the deathlike sleep of total exhaustion. No dreams animated her repose. The chill mists that arose in the hours before dawn failed to disturb her. Only when the sun finally pushed its way above the peaks that loomed all around did she awaken.

"If the blizzard of a week ago hadn't been followed by unseasonable warmth, you would have frozen to death last night," Erimenes chided her as she sat up. "I'll thank you to be more cautious in the future. It wouldn't do for me to be stranded among these tedious valleys."

"Why the concern over my welfare?" Moriana asked. Erimenes gave the same answer as when she had questioned him before about his new solicitousness: silence. *Maybe he's afraid of being stuck here for generations, with nothing to entertain him but the ponderous circling of the seasons.* But that explanation failed to satisfy her.

"I congratulate you on the resourcefulness with which you handled those abominable birds," Erimenes said. "It would have been too degrading to contemplate had one of them swallowed my jar. Imagine spending the rest of the monster's natural life—and in past years they were renowned for their longevity—rolling about inside its gizzard with a lot of common pebbles and the occasional bone. Brrr."

Her every joint feeling like an unoiled hinge, Moriana rose and went to the stream. Kneeling, she splashed water on her face, gasping as the stinging cold revived her. She shook her head, sending droplets glittering off in the early sun. She finally realized Erimenes was speaking to her.

"Pardon?"

"I said, I've decided I'm not at all dismayed at the present turn of events. You're much more stimulating that that slugabed Fost. For one thing your nicely rounded posterior as you bend over the creek . . ."

"Fost!" Moriana's startled cry interrupted the spirit. "I must find out what happened to him." She settled on her knees and began the scrying spell, her hand poised above the stream.

"Are you sure you want to?" Erimenes's words sounded strangely gentle. "Remember the odds he faced." He didn't say, *Remember what awaited him if he was captured by Rann,* and Moriana marveled at his restraint. She continued the chant.

The water went murky, roiled and became a window. Sun rays slanted across a high rock face honeycombed with black holes. Huge shaggy shapes lumbered across the steppe in front of a high cliff.

"Look!" Moriana cried. She seized the satchel, dragged it to her and pulled out Erimenes's jug, uncapping it in the throes of her excitement. "Look, Erimenes. He lives!"

Blue mist arose from the jar. It gyrated briefly, coalesced into the familiar gaunt figure. Erimenes bent forward to peer myopically into the water.

"He does indeed," the spirit said, as violence suddenly swept the tableau. "But for how long?"

Moriana could only shake her head, her features a mask of impotent worry.

Fost watched the copper band of sunlight expand across the steppes as the sun rose over the distant Gulf of Veluz. He breathed deeply of the clear, brisk air and felt his body tremble, both from the weakness caused by his wounds and anticipation of what was to come.

"The Sun Bear rolls the Great Globe into the sky," the shaman intoned. "The time has come."

Silently the People of Ust rose from their campfires and went to the hulking, reeking shapes of their mounts tethered by the domelike tents. Following them, Fost nursed doubts as to the truth of what the shaman said. From what he had heard, he didn't think the time would ever come to challenge a sorcerer such as Kleta-atelk of the Hurinzyn.

A shirt of mail weighted down his shoulders, its hem

slapping his thighs just above the knees as he walked. A round shield of bearhide rode on his left arm. The unfamiliar hardness of a helmet enclosed his head. For what it was worth, he was well armored. In his experience mere armor seldom had any use against enchantment. His thoughts did not run along optimistic lines.

They turned more morose still when his mount was presented to him. "This is Grutz," Jennas said, slapping the blunt red nuzzle companionably. "His rider, Suss, fell last night with an arrow in her eye. Here, Grutz, behold your new master. Fost is a doughty fighter, if a trifle dim. You'll like him."

Fost failed to appreciate the introduction but felt the time wrong to protest, particularly since the beast looked malevolently at him and growled deep in its throat.

"There," Jennas said in satisfaction. "See? He likes you."

"As appetizer or entrée?" asked Fost.

Jennas guffawed. "You've spirit for a northlander," she said, dealing him a buffet on the shoulder that loosened his teeth. "Irtans and the others are foolish babblers when they say we should have fed you to the bears or let the birdmen finish you."

"I am, of course, grateful for your timely arrival last night," Fost said, "but you seem to assume I'll aid you in your battle against this sorcerer."

"And why not?" Jennas asked. "It is only fitting. We save your thick hide from the birdmen and you aid us. Are we not all children of Ust? Do we not worship the same god? Do we not share the same code of justice given us by the Red Bear of the East?"

"Justice?" Fost croaked weakly, glancing from Jennas to Grutz and back.

"A life for a life. We save you, you must offer your life to the Bear Clan in return. One way or the other."

Fost looked around. Others of the Bear People gathered, fingering knife hilts and smiling more like wolves than bears. Their lumbering mounts rocked restlessly, talons grating against rock. They could as easily slash through his tender flesh.

"You're saying I *must* aid you in exterminating this sorcerer?"

"Of course you *must!*" boomed Jennas. "It is your duty. You owe it to us. After this duty to the clan, the obligation is erased."

"I've had dealings with sorcerers in the past, bad dealings. I want nothing more to do with them."

"Grutz."

Fost retreated and stopped short when he felt a knife blade pricking into his back. The huge bear Jennas had called moved forward with ponderous steps. Its mouth opened to reveal fangs that Fost fancied to be the length of his own fingers.

"Mount and ride, Fost Longstrider."

She didn't have to add, "Or else Grutz sups early."

Fost smiled, hoping Jennas would read the tautness in the expression as bravado. He could think of nothing to say, so he put his foot in the stirrup and tried to hoist himself into the saddle on Grutz's high, sloping back. Fost had difficulty until Jennas put a hand under his rump and boosted him up.

Grutz grunted, shifting under the weight. Fost swayed dangerously, blushing with furious embarrassment. The other bear-riders appeared not to notice how their hetwoman had assisted him. They adjusted the hang of their weapons, fiddled with medicine bags and fetishes or simply stared somberly across the brightening steppes. A group of dispirited helots went about striking the tents and stowing them for the trail. The nomad raiders took their homes with them and left nothing to mark their campsites.

Jennas had mounted her beast, immense and brown with claws like black scythes. She plucked a lance from a rest, waved it above her head and spurred the bear into an eastward waddle. The bear-riders followed, forming up in a long column behind. Fost took his station at the end of the line. Grutz's muscles flowed smoothly under his fur, but his gait was ragged, lurching Fost about until the courier felt as though he were riding an earthquake.

Misery rapidly overtook him. Rationally he should have been far more upset by the desperate eagle ride from the City in the Sky and the twisting, confused aerial battle that could have sent him plunging to inevitable death. But then he had been too busy fighting for his life to indulge in excess emotion. Now, with hours stretching empty before him, he had ample time to spend convincing himself he was about to fall off and break his neck.

In a way that might have been preferable. Last night, stumbling away from the scene of the battle, Fost had heard how the Ust-alayakits, the People of Ust, had chanced to come to his rescue. They warred with a neighboring folk, the Hurinzyn, who dwelled in caves east of the bear-rider's range. The Hurinzyn—badger clan—were ruled by the sorcerer Kleta-atelk, who delighted in producing magical monsters. In days past the hunter-herdsmen of the Bear totem had often warred with the more agriculturally oriented Badgers. Since the advent of Kleta-atelk the conflict had taken on a far more bitter character.

"Whether to feed his pets or for some purpose more hideous," Jennas had told Fost, "his men and his monsters have been raiding our flocks. Of late they have taken children too." Her voice dropped beneath its usual deep contralto. "A week ago my daughter Duri was taken and my freemate Timrik, her father, was slain defending her. Half a score other children of Ust were reaved away as well. So now we ride against the cursed Hurinzyn, to triumph or to die."

Leaving oldsters, children and noncombatant parents to stay behind with the flocks, the fighting strength of the People of Ust, some hundred warriors of both sexes, had set out for Hurinzyn territory the day before. As they camped, their scouts reported a body of bird-riders swooping in a landing at the foot of the mountains. Intent on Fost and Moriana, the Sky City troops hadn't noticed the bear-riders stealing up silently to pin them against the sheer rock walls as thoroughly as they had pent up their own quarry. Just as Jennas had been about to attack, the Guardsmen had rushed Fost's camp. Though in the habit of slaying all strangers, the bear-riders had been impressed by the courage of Fost's solitary stand against such numbers. Still, they had been prepared to let the Guardsmen do the work of finishing off this valiant warrior—until he had called on Ust for aid. The sign had been clear: Ust had provided this outlander to aid his folk against Kleta-atelk. They had unhesitatingly gone forward to his rescue.

Fost had been bandaged, fed and housed in a hide tent stretched over the bones of some colossal creature. In the morning he had been given the best of the spare equipment. Under the circumstances he could scarcely refuse to join the bear-folk on their raid. Yet he fretted as he rode across the flat, featureless land in the lee of the Ramparts. Time fled. Would Moriana wait for him or was she at this very instant nearing Athalau, intent on using the Amulet of Living Flame to help depose her sister?

His fatalistic fury of the night before had gone. Now he looked back on his reckless berserker rage with something akin to shame. He wished he knew more of his antecedents that he might learn whether his family had a history of madness. Life now seemed very precious to him; joining in a desperate expedition against a wizard of surpassing might and wickedness struck him as a poor way to hang onto it.

For all their ungainly bulk the bears rolled along at a pace much quicker than a man could walk. Feeling his breakfast of dried meat and sour bear's milk churning in his stomach, Fost groaned. In action he would have a hard enough time just staying aboard his mount. If Ust had indeed contrived to have him join the attack, the doctrine of divine infallibility was in for a drubbing.

They had ridden two hours when a shout roused Fost from the dour reverie into which he had fallen. Looking up, he saw two figures rise from the grass and flee with a peculiar hunching lope: badgers, slightly smaller than the Ust-alayakits' bears, with black on their masks and limbs. Their riders wore peaked fur caps and long, dirty robes. They showed no signs of armor and carried javelins with bone shafts.

The bear-riders jeered at the retreat of their enemies. Even Jennas shouted after them, her stern, handsome features flushed as though she'd just won a battle.

Did they seriously expect a pair to fight a hundred? Fost wondered. He began to understand his new comrades better. The growing enlightenment failed to cheer him.

The village of the Hurinzyn came into view. The mountains here rose abruptly from the steppe in a grey, shiny wall. Artists or nature had pocked the stone face with a myriad caves in which the badger-folk made their homes. Ledges scaled the cliff in terraces, chiseled out of living rock to provide lateral access between the caves. Vertical movement was accomplished by means of ladders. Warned by their pickets, the badger-folk had drawn up the lowest of these. By any means Fost could see, the homes of the Hurinzyn were unreachable to the People of Ust. The courier wondered if Jennas had some scheme he'd been unable to guess at.

One hole at the highest level was larger than the rest and fronted with a wide balcony of stone, a single broad slab that jutted from the cliff. From the hole emerged a lone figure. He was a tall man, or so Fost surmised, for his back was badly hunched. Wild black hair shot with grey fell around his shoulders and a beard of the same combination reached knobby knees left bare by the smock he wore. His garment was a faded black, crudely embroidered with white and lemon pictographs. He supported himself on a staff carved of yellowing bone topped with a gap-eyed and fanged badger's skull. His own eyes were round ebony glints.

"Kleta-atelk," Jennas said, reining her bear at Fost's side. The bridle applied pressure to the beast's neck to guide it while leaving the jaws free to bite.

"I surmised as much," Fost said. The badger-shaman raised an arm and began to sing in a high, trembling voice. "What's he up to?"

"He chants up his creatures," said Jennas. She cinched her helmet strap tight beneath her jaw.

"Are they otherwordly?"

She shook her head. "He must keep his song to control them. His pets are mortal beasts, 'tis said, transformed to monsters by his sorcery. The change maddens them. Should his chant falter, they'd fall on the Hurinzyn in an instant—and him as well."

More figures sprang from the waist-high grass. A line of Hurinzyn on foot confronted the bear-riders. The unarmored footmen cast javelins. Slings whined and loosed buzzing projectiles. A rock glanced off Fost's shield, momentarily numbing his arm. A grey bear to his left was struck by a spear just in front of its rider's leg. The creature gave no sign of noticing. Less vigorously driven than the spears and arrows of the Sky

Guardsmen had been, the Hurinzyn javelins failed to pierce the coarse fur and fat that sheathed the bears' vitals.

Jennas whipped her greatsword loose from its sling across her back. "Forward!" she shouted. Growling, the column of bears spread into a line and charged. The Hurinzyn skirmishers loosed a desultory hail of missiles and took to their heels.

Fost's worries about controlling his beast proved well founded. No matter how he tried to rein in, Grutz put his massive head down and charged along with his fellows, rumbling deep in his throat like a distant thunderstorm.

"Hold on!" Fost bellowed, clinging to the horn of his pitching saddle. "Stop! Can't you see we're being led into a trap!"

A warrior-woman grinned fiercely at him in passing, whether in contempt at his caution or thinking he gave his battle cry, he couldn't tell. Jennas's big brown ran far in advance of the charge, rolling with all the irresistibility of an avalanche toward the departing badgerfolk.

Just as the animal's jaws gaped to seize a Hurinzyn, the disaster Fost feared came crashing down on the People of Ust.

From burrows dug into the clay erupted monsters. Horrid parodies of natural creatures swarmed over the bear-riders. A thing like a badger but covered with slimy skin grabbed a rider from his saddle. The man screamed as the acid seeping from its pores consumed him. An eight-legged dog ran in front of Fost's mount, slavering in mad rage. Something that seemed all eyes and mucus lashed at him with a jointed sting. He warded off the blow with his shield and swept his blade in a bloody line over the gaping orbs. Grutz carried him headlong.

Suddenly the red bear put his rump to the ground and stopped so precipitously that Fost had to brace his hands against the pommel to keep from being emasculated. Falling back into his saddle, he looked ahead to see what had made the animal halt. Then he turned his head and vomited.

At the foot of the cliffs a *thing* waited. Twice as high as a bear, wide as several, a mass of obscenely white and obese flesh, it sat and raised its voice in a lament. Great dugs drooped like sacks across its bulging belly and arms lay in boneless loops tipped with clumps of yard-long tentacles. Its eyes were wide and blue, long-lashed and weeping constant tears down cheeks and shapeless nose. The mouth had been elongated into a trunk, ending in incongruously red lips.

The apparition had unquestionably once been human. "Taimgring!" The shriek soared above the yammer of battle. "O Ust, it cannot be!"

Jennas's bear had halted and refused to budge. Anticipating the horror's advance, Jennas reslung her sword and seized her lance. At the despairing cry she twisted in her saddle.

A tawny bear lunged past her, slobbering foam in its panic. On its back rode a woman taller than Jennas, with braided black hair flying from her helmet. She plunged her sword into her animal's rump to goad it into motion. "No!" The black-haired woman howled, an explosion of agony. *"My daughter!"*

All action stopped. Even Kleta-atelk's changelings ceased battling to watch the dreadful reunion. The amorphous head turned. The streaming dish-sized eyes saw the demented woman who had lost a child and now found it transformed into the essence of a thousand nightmares. Its arms reached.

Its tentacle-fingers wrapped around its mother and lifted her to its breast. The black-haired woman dropped her weapons and embraced her ghastly child. Then she screamed.

The lips had pressed beneath her breasts as though in a caress of love. They peeled back to reveal sharp, chisellike teeth that cut through mail and skin and ribs with equal ease.

Fost's heels dug into Grutz's side. The red bear coughed and broke into a run. Abashed at having to carry a lowly outlander into battle, Grutz displayed none of his fellows' dread of the once-human monstrosity.

Sucking its mother's entrails into its belly through the tube of its mouth, the behemoth turned its eyes on Fost. A sickening stench wafted from it. Its gelatinous flesh wriggled as it stretched a hand toward the courier.

Grutz roared. Fangs flashed. A squeal of anguish bubbled from the thing. Still feeding on the writhing body of its mother, it tried to wrest its hand from the bear's jaws. Fost's broadsword hacked the arm through. Blood hosed over him.

The monster's keening rose to a petulant crescendo. Fost lunged. His sword tip sundered iron links and struck through the heart of the black-haired woman. Dropping her corpse, the being reached for him. His sword rose high and fell again and again, until the bloated face with its questing, sucking proboscis had been butchered to red ruin. With a final slobbering cry the being flopped to its side, convulsed and died.

The fight had surged to life again as Fost, sick to the depths of his soul, turned Grutz away from the mountain of cooling flesh. Badger-riders had appeared to take the attackers from the flank. With shield and spear the lighter defenders took a heavy toll of the bear-mounted People of Ust, whose formation had been ruptured by the onslaught of the monsters.

"Jennas!" Fost shouted at the sight of the Ust-alayakits' leader. Though her greatsword had slashed their riders down, three grunting badgers held her bear by snout and two legs while the warrior-woman fought a caricature of the beast she rode. Covered with squirming pink tendrils instead of fur, the bear-thing obviously held the upper hand.

Again Grutz charged. Fost smashed in the skull of a badger. Jennas's bear whipped the freed paw around and disemboweled the animal that clung to its nose. The bear-riders' chieftain struck at the final badger with her sword as the monster turned its wrath on Fost.

The round shield was pushed far up Fost's arm, enabling his left hand to grip the saddle horn. He wasn't going to chance falling beneath all those stamping, clawed feet. Unable to shield himself, the courier chose attack and drove his sword into the bear-thing's hanging belly.

The blade became bloodied. The thing's own fat armored it as well as any bear's. Blinking, Fost barely had presence of mind to lean back in the saddle to avoid a sweep of its paw. The talons raked the front of his helmet, skirring jaggedly against the metal.

Fost fought for balance. Grutz backed slowly away from the beast, sparring with it, swiping with his paws. Gashes hatched his shoulders. The monster had a longer reach. Fost shook his head to clear it and raised his sword, steeling himself for a last suicidal lunge into those lethal claws.

A brown battering ram smashed into the bear-thing's side. It went down, squalling and snapping at the splintered end of Jennas's lance, which jutted from its side.

"Come on!" the hetwoman shouted.

Her brown bear galloped away from the cliffs. Fost sent Grutz lumbering after.

"Did I save you or you me?" he asked, dazed.

"I don't know," Jennas flung over her shoulder. "All

I know is that we have lost." Moisture gleamed on her cheeks. On both sides of them the surviving People of Ust turned their mounts and fled.

Behind the routed bear-riders, Kleta-atelk's chant droned like a dirge.

Feeling as weak as if she had fought at Fost's side, Moriana slumped back onto her heels. "He lives," she whispered, wanting to affirm it, hardly daring to believe it.

"Indeed," said Erimenes judiciously. "I believe I've judged the boy too harshly. He put on quite an excellent fight, don't you agree? Especially the way he rescued that buxom wench who appears to lead the bear-folk."

"He could hardly have let the monster kill her!" Moriana snapped. Erimenes smirked. With a weary gesture Moriana dismissed the image.

"What do you intend to do now?" the philosopher asked.

The princess shrugged. "Await Fost here," she said. "I could use the rest, and this valley is fair." She looked at the spirit with sudden suspicion. "No heat-seeking birds lie in wait here, do they?"

"No."

Moriana rose, stretched, felt the wan warmth of the sun on her upturned face. Her duty urged her onward, to forge ahead across the Ramparts and take the amulet for herself. Her need for it was greater than his; all he desired was eternal life for himself, whereas her sole motivation was the welfare of her people.

Now that you know he's alive, you owe him no more, her conscience told her. *Go on.*

She shook the thought away with a toss of her long, blond hair. She had left Fost once, and guilt had nearly crippled her. She wouldn't do it again.

"I'm surprised to find a valley this lovely in these desolate mountains," Moriana remarked. "I wonder if it has a name?"

"It does," Erimenes said. "The Valley of Crushed Bones."

Her head snapped toward him. A spectral arm pointed up the valley. At its head several hundred yards away, the green grass was littered with what appeared to be sticks gleaming whitely in the sun.

CHAPTER
FIVE

gested, rubbing his moustache with the back of his hand. "That would bring us high enough to get a hand-hold on the ledge."

"And what will the Hurinsyn be doing while you're

"Attack without our bears?" the clansman roared. "Impossible!"

Fost scowled, returning the bear-riders' glares in kind. Overhead the sun shone meekly through a high haze. The wind blew from the South, a chilling caress. The false summer had gone, and winter would soon follow.

The abortive assault on the badger clan had confirmed Fost's earlier suspicion. In matters of cunning the Ust-alayakits were competent enough; their trapping of Rann's Guardsmen demonstrated that. But methodical military planning wasn't part of their makeup. If no simple stratagem suggested itself, their response was a headlong charge, and Istu take the hindmost.

It was a phenomenon Fost had noted among other mounted tribes. Nor did the reluctance of the bear-riders to part with their mounts surprise him. The nomads' bears were the central fact of their lives, of war, the hunt and worship. Going into battle in any other fashion except on the backs of the ferocious beasts was, to them, simply inconceivable.

Yet they had to start conceiving of it soon. Or they would have no hope of defeating the Hurinzyn in their cliff dwellings.

"Listen," Fost said. "I ask you again. How do you intend to reach the caves of the badger clan?"

"We can stand on our bears' backs," a man suggested, rubbing his moustache with the back of his hand. "That would bring us high enough to get a handhold on the ledge."

"And what will the Hurinzyn be doing while you're

climbing up? Jabbing you with pikes and dropping great whacking rocks on your ugly faces, that's what. You can count on it." Fost waved his hand contemptuously. "Not that the opportunity would ever arise. You were in that charge as well as I. The Hurinzyn light cavalry and Kleta-atelk's atrocities would rip you to shreds before you got within javelin-cast of the cliff."

"Aye, we were in the charge," a scar-faced blond woman spat, "and well we marked who first it was to run from the wizard's beasts. You're no sending of Ust, outlander; a common coward, I call you. We should take you out for the winged foxes to eat."

"Who was it who gave grace to Iedre, when all else sat and gaped in terror?" Jennas's voice cracked like a whip. She stood aloof from the circle, moodily staring at the distant cliff. The other bear-riders stared at her. None could mistake what was on her mind. The canker of defeat plagued the proud war leader and concern over her daughter's fate wore heavily on her. "Who came to my aid when I was sorely beset by those monsters?"

The nomads looked at one another, shamefaced.

"We may as well admit mere valor won't save our children," Jennas said bitterly. "If the stranger suggests new and troublesome ways to meet our problem, I ask, why else did Ust send him? Perhaps our thinking has become like a bone broken and improperly set. Perhaps we must break our ways that they may knit and grow strong again."

None opposed her. Those that were too hidebound to accept the suggestions of a foreigner bore too much respect for their hetwoman's strong sword arm to contradict her.

"Very well," said Fost, leaning forward to prop his square chin on the backs of his hands. His elbows lay on his knees, and like the Ust-alayakits, he squatted by a dispirited yellow fire of dried grass and bear droppings. "I propose to scale the cliffs at that landslip five miles from the Hurinzyn's caves. We'll signal you when we reach the heights above their dwellings. You'll attack, Kleta-atelk will emerge to call forth his pets and find us dropping in on him from above. You've ropes with you, don't you?" Jennas nodded. "Good," said Fost, feeling almost pleased at the progress he was making with them.

He stood up gradually, his joints stiff with cold and fatigue. "So who goes with me?" he asked.

No one spoke. He looked around the circle of warriors, male and female. None met his gaze. He sighed. The little progress he felt he'd made slipped away like sand through his fingers.

None of the bear-riders wished to face the disgrace of fighting on foot like a thrall. The raiders were willing to acknowledge the necessity of it, now that a bear-borne assault had proven fruitless. It was just that no one personally wanted any part of it.

Fost decided not to force the issue. The bear-riders who would go with him would be rebellious and resentful. Unbidden, the image of Moriana flickered through his mind. Irritation tautened his nerves. He realized he couldn't stay here among the bear-folk much longer, playing at their war games. What if Moriana went after the amulet without him? His concern was compounded with worry over Moriana and worry over his own prospects of immortality. In what proportion he couldn't easily decide.

"If that's the way you want it," he said heavily, "then I'll look elsewhere for my storming troops." He turned to Jennas. "Have somebody bring me the senior among your helots."

* * *

Uttering its hunting cry, a hollow, dismal moan, the vast shape of the winged fox spun across the colorless sky and dropped, wings folding to its side. Teetering on the knife-edge of a hogsback, Fost watched the creature drop into the grey shadows at the bottom of a ravine. Below, a dog-sized shape fled with rapid, agile bounds, dodging and weaving around boulders to throw the hunter off its aim. The flyer descended on its prey, and its wings covered the running beast.

"The thulyakhashawin falls on its prey from above," said Ixrim from behind Fost. "We'll do likewise?"

Fost turned back to see the gnarled little helot grinning at him with a set of teeth as incomplete as Prince Rann's morals. The man's hair looked grey beneath the grime that coated him from toes to crown, and one eye watched the world through the milky film of a cataract. A more unprepossessing sight Fost had seldom seen. Yet Ixrim was neither the best nor the worst of the score of thralls he led. He grunted and set off.

The outlander had yet to unravel the relationship between the lordly bear-riders and their helots. The slaves lived in abject misery and filth, subsisting on scraps thrown them by their overlords. Yet the ragged helots were trained by their masters in the use of arms and had been known to fight savagely in defense of the bear-riders' camps. In Fost's experience slaveowners were obsessed with keeping their human chattel unarmed for fear of servile revolt. Somehow the concept of turning against their owners had never dawned on the bear-riders' helots. He had met no resistance from the bear-folk at his suggestion that he take a party of armed slaves for his assault on the Hurinzyn's caves.

The slaves had been promised their freedom if their attack succeeded, a prospect they had greeted with apparent apathy. One of the bear-folk had told Fost the helots were both sons and daughters of slaves and captives taken in raids. As far as the outlander could tell, the possibility of becoming a slave was an implicit part of the steppe nomads' culture, which they accepted with resignation if captured. He wondered if the strapping, buxom Jennas could ever meekly consent to being another's property. He doubted it.

"Master." At the timid voice from behind he turned, missed his footing on a loose rock and flapped his arms to keep from pitching off the narrow trail into the depths of either side. His right leg ached abominably. The stab-wound Rann had dealt him had been superficial, and Jennas's healing magics had done much to mend it overnight. But the climbing and walking hadn't done the injured limb any good.

"What is it?" he asked, more gruffly than he'd intended. Recovering his balance, he stooped and began massaging his bandaged thigh.

The speaker was a woman, ageless in her rags and filth, who carried a hide shield and a hand ax. As with their owners, helots of both sexes bore arms.

"Kleta-atelk is a sorcerer of great power," she said, her voice a monotone, as if the question she asked and the answer she received, whatever its portent, were of only the mildest interest. "How shall we defeat him?"

Fost was none too sure of the details himself, trusting to his own resources to provide a solution at the appropriate time. Plans too closely laid tended to go far awry where magicians were concerned, even mad hunchbacked tribal shamans. His assault along the cliff tops was simply meant to bring him in striking distance of the sorcerer.

"I'll say his name backward," he said, grinning. The woman's expression remained blank. After a moment his own smile faded and he limped on. In the depths of the ravine to his right, the winged fox tore at the body of its prey.

The sun had fallen halfway down the western sky when they stumbled across the Hurinzyn pickets. Fost had lapsed into blank reverie, his mind numbed by the herbs Jennas had given him that morning to soothe his leg. He reacted a fraction of a second too late when a figure sprang from the rocks ahead and lunged at him with a bone-tipped javelin.

The javelin caught him full in the chest. He gasped, staggered back and sat down battling for breath. His mail shirt had stopped the point, but the force of the blow stunned him. Flaps of his fur cap flaring, the Hurinzyn lunged at Fost with his javelin poised for the kill.

Someone hurled past the choking courier. A shield turned the javelin, and an ax licked out to split the badger-clansman's cap and skull. He fell. Other Hurinzyn had emerged from the rocks and struggled with the helots. As Fost got to his feet, he saw his benefactor turn to him and smile. It was the black-haired woman who had spoken to him earlier. A javelin transfixed her throat. Fost stared at her as she collapsed, wondering why she smiled.

The fight was done. A half dozen bandy-legged Hurinzyn lay dead with two of the helots. Shaking his head to rid himself of a feeling of unreality, Fost led the party onward.

They had long since left the treacherous hogsbacks and walked along on the tops of the cliffs into which the badger-people had dug their homes. Glancing over the edge, Fost saw the terraces of the Hurinzyn village not a quarter of a mile ahead. No signs of unusual activity showed. No one had heard the brief combat.

Keeping back from the rim, Fost and his helots moved forward. The clifftop was a shelf of rock a hundred yards across that rose sharply on the far side to merge with the mountain's flank. Boulders the size of

the bear-riders' tents littered the broad ledge. Fost led
the way into a cluster of rocks he judged nearest to
Kleta-atelk's cave. Motioning them to stay in place, he
crept forward and peered over the verge. Below and to
the right was an outcrop of rock that marked the sorcerer's dwelling-place.

Fost looked around. A number of sizable rocks lay
nearby. The first glimmerings of an idea came to him.
He smiled.

He returned to the helots, who huddled among the
boulders without speaking. They had acquitted themselves well enough against the Hurinzyn sentries, but he
was glad there'd been no serious fighting yet. He uprooted a dead shrub, carried it to the edge of the cliff
and drew out his flint and steel.

He had just set the bush on fire when a wild scream
brought him round. The bush flared amid tan smoke,
the signal to the bear-riders to commence their diver-
sionary attack. Fost forgot it as he saw the cause of the
desperate cries. The peculiar, fecal reek of one of Kleta-
atelk's playmates rolled across Fost's palate. His sword
rasped free of its scabbard.

One of the boulders had come to life—or so it
seemed for an instant. The thing was as big as a boulder but its hue was a shiny, bluish white, the color of a
drowning victim. Obscenely glistening tentacles waved,
as fat and pale as maggots and as thick as his thigh. He
watched one of the tentacles curl around the waist of a
helot and lift him into the air. Great suckers sprouted
like concave mushrooms from the back of the moist
bulk. The thrashing helot was brought down close to
them. The suckers clutched his flesh and clung horribly.
The man went stiff in agony.

Stillness fell, shroudlike. Fost and the helots watched,
stunned, as the man's face contorted, purpled and
seemed to fall in on itself like a collapsing tent. At the

same time his body shriveled. With a rippling, smacking sound the tentacles pulled the empty husk from its multiple mouths and tossed it away. Blood drooled from the suckers.

A spear drove into the monster's side. Black ichor jetted out with a reek that contracted Fost's nostrils and caught at the back of his throat. Their apathy gone, the thralls hurled themselves against the horror, hacking at its tentacles and jabbing its bloated side.

Keening, the monster fought back. Its tentacles swooped like serpents, coiling around the helots and dashing them to lifeless rags against the rocks. Fost saw Ixrim seized, his dark face set in lines of determination as he sawed with his sword at the member holding him. The blade cut through rubbery flesh, causing the tip of the tentacle to fall way in a gush of corruption, but other tendrils lashed in to trap the wiry little helot. He was still resisting grimly as the suckers met his belly with a kiss that sucked the vitals from his body.

Down on the plain the bear-riders must be attacking the Hurinzyn again, Fost thought, and it seemed to him that he could hear the drone of Kleta-atelk's chant. The Ust-alayakits could fight the enchanter's monsters for only a short time before they were overwhelmed. He had to act fast to defeat the shaman in time to aid them.

But he had already stood by while slaves sold themselves as dearly as any free folk. He could stand by no longer. He raised his sword and approached the horror.

Tentacles dipped toward him, to fall writhing like snakes as his basket-hilted broadsword cut them through. The monster's cries of agony rose to an intolerable pitch, but still Fost came on, swinging his blade until he waded knee-deep through slimy black foulness.

Then he was beside the pulsating fat body of the

thing. He cocked his arm to drive the sword to the hilt. From behind the bulk, like a sun rising, came a Face.

It was a face of unearthly beauty, shining with a golden light. A high-cheeked, full-lipped androgynous face smiled in invitation. Fost looked into its eyes, great orbs of amber. The strength drained from his limbs.

"You are different," the Face said. "Unlike these twisted rabbits. Your limbs are strong and straight, your chest broad, your face alive with arrogance." The lips smiled. They gleamed like moist jewels. "I would love you, outlander."

Fost's veins swelled with desire. It was as if the Face existed alone, discrete from the obscene bloated mass that was its body. The Face embodied all that he desired. His manhood burgeoned at his loins.

Tentacles enveloped him, caressing, beguiling. He let them urge him forward. Their tips, facile and as dainty as a maiden's fingers, undid the thongs that sealed his breeches to peel the garment away.

A coral tongue made a lascivious circuit of the lips. "I would taste your flawless manhood, feel your virility flow into me. Come, come unto me, my love." Lust and adoration glowed in the eyes.

The lips waited, subtly parted. Desire filled Fost, but a small voice of rebellion spoke within him. *Illusion!* it cried. *Beware!* Yet he couldn't believe it. Within the circle of those red, red lips awaited beauty and satiation.

Then he saw the gleam of sunlight on a tooth like a dagger's blade.

"Come," urged the Voice. "Give me your masculinity. Impale me with your hardness!" And Fost obeyed.

The eyes closed ecstatically as his hips moved forward. But his arm moved too, and the eyes shot wide again as the tip of his sword sliced through the perfect lips, cleaved the pink tongue and punched out the back of the creature's neck. Rage blazed in its eyes. Its scream spattered Fost with blood. Then a dying spasm of the maggot-pale tentacles cast him away.

He slammed into the ground, rolled over and lay retching until his stomach knotted spastically on nothing. His sword was still in his hand, the blade smeared with stinking black ichor. He glanced down and saw that his arm, the front of his body and the limp worm of his penis lolling across his thigh were all drenched with the foul stuff. He tried to vomit again but his belly had already emptied itself.

Thirty feet away the monster jerked in its death throes. The head hung to one side and the ruined face was slack. The survivors of the assault group crawled away from the dying thing. Its blood fell on them like black rain.

Gagging, Fost pushed himself to his feet. A monotonous chant penetrated the bleariness of his skull and brought about a sense of urgency. *Kleta-atelk!* He staggered toward the edge of the cliff.

He swayed dizzily on the lip of the precipice. Grinding teeth into lower lip to focus his mind, he looked down. Out on the steppe a battle raged. Hulking shapes, indistinct with distance but obviously unnatural, fought with a pitiful few bear-riders. Gradually the monsters pushed the Ust-alayakits back. Fost saw Jennas, embattled and alone, laying about her with her greatsword. Badger-riders circled her, closing in as monsters tried to drag down her bear. She held her own, but the outcome was inevitable and couldn't long be forestalled.

"Omnegallillagall, Ulltip, nasripul, zazzigazz ra!" The flow of syllables, nonsense to Fost, brought his attention to a point only yards under his boots. Kleta-atelk stood on his ledge, hunched against his skull-tipped staff, peering through round lenses of black glass

as he sang his song of control. He must have heard the sounds of conflict so near above his head but he ignored them, trusting to the guardian horror he had left on the clifftops to deal with intruders.

Weak as a newborn child, Fost bent down. His fingers grasped a rock twice the size of his head. Groaning, he swung it high. A twitch of the sorcerer's crooked shoulders showed that he had sensed the presence above him, but he wouldn't be distracted from his song.

And then it was too late. The rock smashed his head into jelly.

An oil lamp burned yellow and wavering inside Jennas's tent. From outside came the sound of merriment as the bear-riders celebrated their victory. A constrained tone underlay their revelry. The price had been high.

Bathed, bandaged and somewhat restored, Fost lay on a bed of furs, drinking freely of heady yellow wine. Across the tent Jennas sat in a folding camp-chair. A child sat on the floor of the tent, slumped against her booted calf. It was a girl-child, not yet blooming into adolescence. She regarded the courier with immense indigo eyes. There was a haunting in those orbs but it faded almost as Fost watched. The girl had seen horror but being young would soon forget. Being not so young, Fost couldn't forget. He gulped down his wine and replenished the emptied goblet from a skin hung from a tentpole.

Her hand lightly stroking the close-cropped plush of the girl's head, Jennas watched him. Golden highlights from the lamp danced in her eyes. On her face showed pity, but also admiration.

"You destroyed Kleta-atelk and freed the land of monstrous evil," she said, sipping moderately from her own goblet. "You saved the children of the Ust-alayakits

—among them my own Duri." The girl glanced up gravely at her mother, who smiled in return, not even resembling the bear-riding Amazon who had earlier been sundering Hurinzyn bodies with single sweeps of her greatsword. "Truly you were sent by Ust."

Fost grunted. He gazed into the wine, saw images there that made him squeeze his eyes shut and shuddered in revulsion. He felt soiled to the center of his soul.

For a time Jennas sat, hand on Duri's head, watching Fost. Outside, the celebration waned as exhaustion set in. The bear-riders returned to their own tents or drifted to the cliff dwellings. To the Ust-alayakits' astonishment the Hurinzyn had welcomed them as liberators after the fall of Kleta-atelk. His magic had held them subservient, though he experimented on their living bodies and fed them to the nightmares he created. Their raids against their neighbors, the bear-folk, had arisen from the shaman's grim pronouncement: he would have his victims and cared little how he came by them. The Hurinzyn stole the Ust-alayakits' children to preserve their own. The bear-folk would take indemnity, of course, but having experienced the evil power of Kleta-atelk themselves, they bore the badger-clan surprisingly little malice. Some of the raiders had already paired off with some of the conquered tribesfolk, and now retired to conduct further celebration in private.

Eventually Jennas reached for a small brass bell and rang it twice. The hide flap of the tent opened promptly to admit an aged helot woman. "The little one has had a long day," Jennas told the servant. "See her bedded down, Unphaia." The hetwoman bent to kiss her daughter on the forehead. Then, clucking, the old woman herded the girl out of the tent and off to bed.

Fost sat staring obliviously into his cup, concentrating on keeping his mind white and empty. A touch on his shoulder made him start.

Jennas stood over him. Even in his numbed state, he was aware how splendid and barbaric she looked, the gold circlets around her brawny arms, heavy gold loops dangling from her ears and her shapeless garb of fur and hide not managing to hide the ripeness of her figure. The lamplight turned her skin to bronze.

"If you turn inward, you won't come out, my friend," she said. Her fingers stroked down his arm.

He raised his hand to hers, meaning to pluck it away, sickened by the very touch. He paused, fingers hovering over the back of her strong hand. *Don't blame her,* a mental voice told him. *She wasn't responsible for the blandishments of Kleta-atelk's guardian—nor the way you responded to them.*

His hand closed on hers in a desperate grip. She knelt. Her breath was warm on his cheek, honeyed by the wine. She kissed his ear. He snatched his head away as though her lips burned him.

She put a hand to his jaw and forced him to face her. The lamp's glow turned her pillow-soft, but she was immensely strong, perhaps as strong as he. Though he tried to resist, he shortly found himself looking into her eyes.

"When our young are taught to ride, sometimes they are thrown and hurt by accident and become afraid," she said gently. "We make them mount again promptly and ride, lest their initial fear stay with them always." She kissed him on the lips. He did not respond, but neither did he draw away. He clung fiercely to her hand, the only anchor he could find in a chaotic world.

"I know what befell you today. The thralls told me." She took his hand and laid it on her breast.

The flesh was warm and vibrant with life. Her heart beat powerfully and fast beneath his fingers. Slowly she drew his hand down until his fingers slid into her jerkin and touched her nipple. Her other hand slipped from his face and began unlacing his tunic. She kissed him again, and he returned it. Her tongue was strong and carried the taste of wine.

His tunic opened. Jennas turned her attention to her own belt. Then her fingers groped for Fost's crotch. He moaned and tried to draw away. Leaving his hand clutching her breast as fervently as it had earlier clutched her hand, she grabbed the back of his neck and crushed his face to hers. Her other hand worked vigorously up and down.

In spite of himself Fost was becoming aroused. He kneaded the handful of her breast, marveling at its firmness. He squeezed her thumb-thick nipples. She moaned and undulated against him.

Her mouth parted from his. Her head dropped, her short red hair tickling down his stomach. He gasped and arched his back as her lips enfolded the head of his trembling manhood.

Unbidden, the Face appeared behind his eyes, lips parted, teeth agleam. With a strangled shout, he tore himself from Jennas's embrace and rolled off the pile of furs.

Jennas leaped to her feet. The short leather skirt she had donned after the battle fell from her hips, leaving her naked from the waist down. The fur of her sex was a vertical red-orange bar, pointing down between smooth, muscular thighs. One brown-tipped breast protruded from the front of her jerkin, jiggling to the angry rhythm of her breathing. Her eyes blazed.

"Be that way then!" she raged at Fost. "Be like a timid virgin boy, afraid of your own appetites! Go and become a Josselit, for all I care!"

"Jennas, I . . ."

"Enough of words! You fought like a man today—

claim your reward like one now." Contempt edged her voice. "Or did Ust send us a eunuch for a champion?"

His head fogged with wine and unwilling passion, Fost got unsteadily to his feet. "You can't talk to me like that."

She slapped him. His head rocked and lights flickered inside his skull. He reeled back, blinking and rubbing his cheek.

When his vision cleared, his jaw slumped in amazement. The hetwoman had thrown herself down on all fours on the furs, presenting her naked hindquarters to him. Her buttocks were sculpted hillocks of muscle. The pink lips of her vulva lay open, inner secretions reflecting the light like a jewel. The thick, urgent odor of her excitement filled his nose and set his heart beating even faster.

"Well?" she asked. The word was a challenge. She confronted him with a choice· Take her or become a monk.

She's right, you know, the courier thought. A bestial growl rose from his throat as his brief anger dissolved into passion. He dropped to his knees, laid hands on her buttocks. The flesh was like soft, warm marble. He throbbed with unbearable tension. Shaking with lust, he thrust forward.

Jennas uttered a guttural exclamation of exultation as his manhood filled her.

"I simply cannot see why you waste time mooning about this dreary valley." Erimenes fluttered spectral hands in exasperation. "Why trouble yourself over Fost? Forget him. The key to everlasting life lies within your grasp. Take it. You can seize the City in the Sky, and with your beauty and power enjoy an unending succession of far more skilled lovers."

"I wish you wouldn't go on so," Moriana said, glancing in irritation at the spirit. "You're just bored." She began pacing to and fro by the campfire.

"Indeed I am, as any sensible soul would be in such tediously bucolic surroundings." He crossed an arm over his chest and laid elbow in palm. He tapped fingers against his chin, an action Moriana found disconcerting, since both fingers and chin lacked substance. Then he brightened. "The time needn't be a total waste though. You could amuse yourself—and me—by engaging in self-stimulation. There's ample wood about. You could carve yourself a dildo of heroic proportions and . . ."

"Enough!" snapped Moriana. She laid elbow in palm and tapped her own chin in unconscious imitation of the sage. "I wonder how Fost fares."

"You know the great oaf lives, at any rate. Why, he positively seems to have covered himself in glory." A sly look stole across the wispy blue features. "Forget him, I say. It's for your own good. You saw the way that she-bear of a hetwoman cast covetous eyes on him, and her with mammaries the size of crystal balls! He's reveling this minute, my lady, with never a thought for you."

Moriana rounded on him, hair flying. "That's not true!"

"Prove me wrong." Erimenes smirked. "Employ your scrying spell."

Moriana chewed her lip for a moment, staring at Erimenes, who assumed a look of such lugubrious and obviously false concern for her welfare that she almost refused. But curiosity nagged at her. What *was* her lover doing? He wasn't the most continent man she'd ever known, and that red-haired hetwoman was definitely handsome in a coarse, emphatic way. Nor was Erimenes—damn his vaporous eyes!—in error about the way she looked at Fost. Moriana paced a minute more, then went to the nearby stream and dropped to her knees.

"I don't doubt they'll adopt him into their clan," said Erimenes, his voice drifting over her shoulder. "He'll marry the chieftainess and raise up a brood of squalling, hirsute brats. Each spring he and she will ride off to the raid together, with matching bear skulls adorning their heads. Ahh," he sighed loudly, "a charming picture."

Moriana's ears burned furiously as she hurried through the words of the spell. The water stirred and grew luminous.

"I'll show you, Erimenes," she flung back at the spirit. "Fost will not betray my trust. He'll spurn that husky slut . . ."

Her words trailed off as an image coalesced.

"Your definition of 'spurn' and mine differ, lady," Erimenes said judiciously, leaning forward to peer into the water.

It required a moment for the princess's eyes to adjust to the gloom of the picture. It took more time for her mind to make sense of what she saw. A woman on elbows and knees, a man kneeling behind her on his knees. . . .

She realized what she was looking at and breath hissed inward.

"She seems to find his spurning most salubrious," Erimenes said.

In stony silence Moriana plunged her hand into the water, dispelling the image. She stood and looked at the spirit's wavering form. Her eyes were like green metal.

"We leave in the morning," she said.

CHAPTER
SIX

bird-riders spent two and a half weeks combing empty grassland without result. When they drew near the Ramparts, they ran the risk of encountering the winged foxes. Rann had lost four men to the beasts.

Stretching, Moriana emerged from the tent. It was of light, oiled skins stitched together and could be rolled small enough to fit in Fost's knapsack. Shivering in the chill dawn, Moriana thanked fortune she had it.

A light fall of snow had dusted the valley, draining color and contrast from the landscape. Large flakes fluttered down. She hugged herself, blew fog from her lips and shook out her hair. At least the snow hid the ominous scattering of bones at the head of the long valley.

"Are we ready to move on yet?" Erimenes inquired from within the tent. "This dismal valley was dull enough to begin with. Now it's cold and damp as well. Let's move."

Teeth chattering, Moriana glanced at the tent. "Why should the cold and damp bother you? You're snug in that nice, warm jug. Brrr."

"Snug? I'd call this intolerably cramped." The scholar's complaints had an unusually bitter tone this morning. "You cannot conceive how dreary it is within this wretched pot. Would that I had a body again!"

Moriana stooped and reentered the tent to wrap her heavy cloak around her shoulders. "Do you mean that? You're immortal, Erimenes. Would you truly trade that for corporeal existence—the discomfort, the transience?"

"What good is immortality if one cannot truly live? To feel, to love, to experience!"

"I thought you got all those through others." She sat on her bedroll and brought out the magic gruel bowl and began to eat the bland porridge.

"You think so?" Erimenes asked scornfully. "What

137

would you rather do, make love to a lusty, well-endowed young buck—or watch another do it?"

Moriana laughed uneasily, her mind darting to what the scrying spell had shown her the night before. Her last spoonful of gruel seemed to curdle in her mouth. She forced it down and made herself think of other things.

The Valley of Crushed Bones was foremost in her mind. The day before, she'd spent fretting about Fost, summoning up scryings in the water and watching until she grew too upset to look any more, pacing like a beast in a pen and then dropping to her knees by the water to make the spell again. She hadn't ventured far up the narrow valley.

Her lack of exploration, she admitted to herself, grew as much from trepidation as concern for Fost—which, she now assured herself, had been misplaced. Those bones, those bleached, broken bones . . . what did they signify?

For all that he had spoken ominously of the Valley before, it seemed Erimenes knew little of it but the name. Perhaps a glacier had come this way and uprooted some ancient burial ground in passing, then retreated, leaving bones strewn about the Valley. Moriana doubted that explanation. She knew how glaciers had advanced across the once-temperate lands that men now called the Southern Waste to swallow ages-old Athalau. She'd never heard of glaciers retreating in the region though. Where the ice once took hold, it clung.

If nothing else, the bonefield was the last serious obstacle between Moriana and Athalau, except for the glacier itself in which the city lay entrapped. The Ramparts didn't soar as high here as they did around the Gate of the Mountains. The walls of the Valley of Crushed Bones rose abruptly to become sheer faces of rock, the flanks of two mighty peaks. At the top of the

Valley the walls closed to within twenty yards of each other in a narrow pass. And beyond, the land lay downward, down to the City in the Glacier.

She ate her fill, for she wished to be well nourished in case the solution to the enigma of the Valley proved a continuing danger. Finishing, she stowed the bowl and took down the tent, packing it away as well. Erimenes grumbled all the while, but his comments didn't seem directed at her. She paid him no mind.

At last she was ready to proceed. She stood with the knapsack slung over her shoulder, gazing up the Valley. The snow had stopped. The day lay still and white beneath a low, grey sky. She sighed and started walking.

Guilt nibbled at the edges of her mind. *I'm abandoning Fost again,* she thought, but immediately *He abandoned me!* flashed through her mind. *The way he rutted with that redheaded slut!*

She shook her head. Better to contemplate the nearness of her goal. Reaching the city without Fost would be a boon, for it meant there would exist no question as to who should possess the amulet. Moriana felt something very much like love for the courier—*or at least I did,* she mentally amended—but it couldn't compare to her love for the City that was her home.

Synalon. The name burned like an ember in her mind. Moriana recalled the scenes of brutality and repression she had witnessed in her beloved City, both in person and by means of her spells. Nor would her sister rest content with imposing an iron yoke on the people of the City. She meant to restore the Sky City's dominion over the Sundered Realm.

Could she accomplish it? Moriana didn't doubt she could. Synalon's sorcerous powers were great, even though the aid of Istu was denied her, for that part of the Sleeper's mind she could tap into would react with venomous hatred to the being that had summoned it up only to cause it consummate agony. And the military might of the City, though not large in terms of manpower, was formidable. Without venturing far from their randomly-floating fortress, the Sky Citizens could control the Great Quincunx that covered the very heartland of the Realm. From Lake Wir to the Southern Steppe, from the Gulf of Veluz to the Thails, the City could dominate the vital trade arteries of the continent.

What her sister would do with all the Realm under her command was something Moriana shrank from considering. Synalon had already shown herself willing to dabble in the dark and grisly rites of the ancients. With all the wealth and populace of a continent, who knew what she could do? Send ten thousand highborn virgins to shrieking impalement upon the stony member of the Vicar of Istu to win the demon's aid and forgiveness? Assuredly Synalon was capable of it. Release black Istu from his millennia-long durance and subject the world once again to the foulness of the Demon of the Dark Ones? Moriana shuddered. Her sister wouldn't balk at such a thing. And with the resources of the Realm at her disposal, perhaps she could succeed even in undoing the work of Felarod the Great.

Moriana raised her head to face the icy blast that blew down the Valley. She could go on alone now with no regrets. She had reminded herself of the gravity of her quest; to succeed, no sacrifice was too great.

The Valley rose at a gradually increasing angle. Before long, Moriana found the going difficult. Snow had made the dead grass slippery. Head down, she scrambled upwards, buffeted by the wind until her feet flew from beneath her and she went face first into the snow.

Grabbing wildly for support, her fingers closed around something smooth and hard. Turning over and sitting up, she brought the object up to examine.

"Gods!"

"There you have why this is known as the Valley of *Crushed* Bones," Erimenes said.

The thing in Moriana's hand was a sunbleached human bone, probably a femur. One end had been splintered by some awful force. Normally anything but squeamish, Moriana was horrified by her prize and flung it far away from her. It rebounded off the looming wall of the canyon with a loud clatter.

Picking herself up, Moriana surveyed the ground ahead. The cliffs were vertical here, save for the huge protrusions of what looked like pink granite humped against the base of either face.

"At least you won't have to wade through the snow for a while," Erimenes observed. Moriana sucked in her cheeks, staring pensively ahead.

The spirit was correct. For a hundred yards the ground was bare. Not bare merely of snow but of vegetation, large rocks and the bone fragments strewn all around where the princess stood. It was as if the stretch of ground were regularly graded and cleared.

"A puzzle," said Erimenes. Dubiously Moriana started forward. A skull turned beneath her boot and threw her against a wall. She put her hand up only to snatch it back. Gingerly she reached out to touch the wall again.

"Erimenes, it's warm," she said. "The rock is warm."

"There is much volcanic activity in these mountains," the philosopher said. "Doubtless what you feel is the very world's lifeblood running through the veins of the rock."

Moriana glanced at the satchel. What he said was possible. It would certainly explain the lack of snow in the pass. Though why it gave the appearance of being swept clean was another matter.

"Hist!" called the spirit. "Something comes!"

From the shallower slopes of the Valley behind broke the hunting cry of a mountain cat. Moriana spun, back to the wall, curved Sky City sword in her hand. Unlike the sightless birds, a big cat was unlikely to attack a human. Unless the onset of winter had made its food scarce. . . .

In an explosion of flying snow a creature raced out of the Valley and passed Moriana. A large rodent with huge, triangular ears pressed to its neck bounded on great hind legs. Hot on its trail and squalling its fury came a tufted-eared cat, its sleek white hide dappled with dark brown to match the incomplete snowy carpet of early winter. Fangs the length of a dirk glinted in its maw, but it paid Moriana no heed as it lunged past.

Onto the bare earth of the pass it pursued the rodent. A rumble resounded in the narrow gap. A ripple passed over the rough, pink surface of the twin protrusions and they seemed to change color before Moriana's startled eyes. Then with a crushing, rending roar they surged together like giant jaws.

As the rocky juts hurtled inwards, the rodent stopped, frozen with fear. The cat sprayed dirt as it sat on its haunches and tried to reverse its course. For all the feline speed of its reflexes, it acted too late. The pink granitelike masses slammed into one another. The crash of their meeting overwhelmed the cat's last defiant cry.

"Saints of blood and darkness," Moriana whispered. "The rock lives!"

"So it would seem," Erimenes said, unperturbed. "I had heard hints of such things, side effects of the War of Powers, but had never encountered any at such close range. Fascinating."

The rock, if rock it truly was, pulsated now, veins of darker color emanating from the spot where the stone mandibles met. A sudden convulsion of the living stone ejected a scatter of white fragments. Moriana gasped in horror as the crushed bones of the rodent and predator were cast into the snow at her feet.

"Now we know the origin of the crushed bones," said Erimenes with a certain satisfaction.

Moriana stumbled a few steps down the slope and sat in the snow. Her head whirled. *A few steps more,* she thought, *that's all it would have taken. Then it would be my bones that lie there, crushed and sucked clean.*

Snow began to fall. Moriana sat hugging her knees, paying it no mind. At last a peevish complaint from Erimenes roused her. She rose, dusted white powder from her thighs and regarded the stony jaws. They had slid back into place. They now looked like nothing more than rounded outcroppings of rock, save for the fact that snow melted as soon as it touched them.

Moriana's eyes rose up the rock walls that flanked the pass. The sheer, smooth faces offered no handholds. High up on the right-hand face she saw an irregularity that might have been a ledge, or no more than a trick of the swirling snow. She shook her head. Even if it was a ledge, she had no way of reaching it.

"We're stymied," she said at last, gathering her cloak more closely around her to ward off the chill. "This passage through the mountains is blocked; the only other I know of is the Gate, far to the East." She clenched her fists in angry disappointment. "I may as well surrender to Rann now as try to reach the Gate of the Mountains across the open steppe."

"Surely you aren't so easily defeated!" Erimenes cried. "You are a woman of great resource. Can't you conceive of some way to get past the monster?"

The passion in the spirit's voice took her aback. He seemed as feverish to reach Athalau as she. What motivated him? Was it merely homesickness, a longing to see his birthplace after almost a millennium and a half of separation? Or was it something else?

Whatever his reasons, they can't be as urgent as my own, she thought. Aloud she asked sarcastically, "What would you have me do? Do you think I can run faster than the rock-leaper or the tufted cat? Do you think I can scale the walls like a spider or would you simply have me sprout wings and fly over this carnivorous canyon to Athalau? Would you . . ." Her voice dwindled into thoughtful silence.

"Well?" demanded Erimenes. "Have you thought of a spell to turn yourself into a bird?"

"No, you garrulous puff of smog. If such magic was in my power, wouldn't I have used it long ago?" She settled the knapsack more firmly across her shoulders, cinching tightly the strap that held Erimenes's satchel. "But perhaps I needn't fly to get over this obstacle."

With that, she ran straight for one of the massive juts. Her momentum carried her several feet up the side of the thing. Her hands and feet scrabbled for purchase, but the monster's rocky hide was slippery. The top of the protrusion was a dozen feet or more above the ground. She had not gotten more than halfway before she began to slip irrevocably backward. A muscular twitch of the animated rock sent her sprawling.

"Are you sure you know no spells of avianthropy?" Erimenes asked.

Ignoring him, Moriana picked herself up and strode purposefully for the outcropping, drawing her sword as she went.

"You don't plan to do battle with the thing?" Erimenes asked in horror.

"What's the matter?" Moriana asked. "Have you lost your taste for gore? No, nebulous one, I don't intend to fight the beast. I do hope to carve us a pathway though." The scimitar slashed twice, a blur of speed.

The thick hide and stony flesh of the monster resisted, but the Sky City blade, its fine blue steel misted by condensation in the cold, cut through both to form a ragged step. The flesh within the wound was yellow and seeped thick red blood.

Moriana hacked another step a foot above the first, and another above that. The great hump of muscle shook convulsively. Syrupy red blood spattered Moriana's face and cloak.

She put her boot in the lowest step. A wild spasm rocked the monster. Her gloved fingers clutched a step, dug in, held.

Clinging with both feet and one hand, hacking with the other, Moriana inched up the flank of the rock monster. When she'd started cutting, the princess had feared the jut would swing back to crush her against the cliff. But apparently the creature was unable to move in any way but back and forth. It could still try to shake her off though, which it did with ever-increasing violence.

Grimly Moriana fought her way upward. She was smeared with the thick blood, and its reek clogged her nostrils. Erimenes shrilled with terror, fearing that at any second she'd be pitched into the monster's maw and be crushed along with his jug. What the destruction of his jar would do to him, Erimenes had no more knowledge than Moriana, and he felt no eagerness to find out.

Then Moriana's head passed the top of the hump and she saw the far slope receding into white oblivion. The creature shook like a dozen earthquakes until Moriana's joints threatened to give way. She held the sword high, plunged it down into the flesh again and then levered herself forward with a powerful shove of her legs. Like a tumbler she somersaulted over the top of the living hump.

Behind her the jaws rammed together again and again with a roar like thunder, as though the monster gnashed its teeth in frustration. For a few breaths Moriana lay on her back, letting the fat white flakes land on her face and melt, spots of stinging coolness on her flushed cheeks. She finally rose and stumbled down the far side of the hill. At her back the jaws of the Valley opened and shut in an avalanche of noise.

Clawed feet scrabbling for traction, the bears made their way along the ledge. Fost's heart lurched each time the slip of a paw on icy rock threatened to send him and Grutz over the edge. The trail would have been perilously narrow going for the broad-beamed beasts under the best of conditions. With the rock sheathed in ice and clouds of snow blinding them, it seemed impossible that the mounts had come this far without slipping to their doom.

In front of him the dimly seen shape that was Jennas turned in her saddle. "Look over the side," she directed. "You'll see why I don't think you'll ever see your woman again."

At her command Fost's stomach turned over. But he made himself crane his neck so he could peer three hundred feet straight down to the valley below. A freak of wind parted the curtain of snow, and he saw clear to the bottom.

He blinked, wondering if the cold played tricks on his eyes. It seemed that the very rock of the cliffs was surging out of both sides of the narrow gorge to slam together in the middle and send a deep rumble shivering up the mountains. It reminded him unpleasantly of giant jaws.

"That's a living creature down there," Jennas said. "It senses when something tries to pass between its jaws, and they slam shut, crushing its prey." She bent dangerously far out of her high-cantled saddle to gaze down. "I've never heard of the monster being so active. Perhaps the blizzard bothers it."

Perhaps it's chewing Moriana's lovely body to a bloody pulp, Fost thought, and instantly regretted it. He cursed his too-vivid imagination.

Jennas twisted to face him again. "Now you've seen what your friend would have had to pass. We know she tried it; I showed you the remnants of her camp back in the Valley of Crushed Bones, and no one else would knowingly enter the vale of the heat-hunters." Her eyes burned like beacons through the snow. "Shall we go on? I did promise to guide you wherever you wished."

Fost's chest expanded within his bearskin cloak as he took a deep, pensive breath. *No,* he thought. *I will not accept that she is dead. Not until I see her corpse.*

The icy air was like razor-sharp knives in his lungs, emotion a dagger in his guts. Was his concern for Moriana alone or for his prospect of recovering the ancient, treacherous shade who alone knew the location of the Amulet of Living Flame? He couldn't answer the question.

The look in his eyes answered Jennas. She set her face into the wind and rode on, leaving the courier to wonder if it was the icy blast that made her eyes water.

Then they were descending to the valley on the far side of the pass. The snow began to thin. Jennas nodded silently as Fost shouted and pointed to a thin spire of smoke corkscrewing into the sky.

They reached the valley floor. Fost booted Grutz to a run, galloping past Jennas's mount and shouting Moriana's name. A slender figure leaped from an overhanging bank and came around the campfire with sword in hand to confront the bear-riders.

"Fost!" Moriana sheathed her sword, and she was running forward too, arms wide. Fost dropped from Grutz's broad back and lunged to meet her. Laughing and shouting with wordless joy, they clung to each other. Moriana babbled the story of her escape from the Valley, running on until Fost stopped her with an embrace.

After an appropriately long kiss, he broke away and turned to Jennas. To his surprise the hetwoman smiled.

"Any woman who can pass through the Valley of Crushed Bones alive is worthy even of a Champion of Ust," she said. "I leave you now. The tents of the Ustalayakits are open to you always." So saying, she turned her bear and loped back toward the trail through the mountains.

Grutz shuffled forward, rumbling deep in his throat. Moriana raised her sword. The great, shaggy head shoved against Fost's chest and nuzzled him. He ruffled the coarse fur of the bear's neck. Then Grutz wheeled and followed the hetwoman of the People of Ust.

Only a few flakes dropped from the leaden sky. Moriana and Fost stood with joined hands, watching as Jennas mounted the trail and ascended with remarkable speed. As she reached the place where the trail disappeared around the mountain, she paused to wave. Fost and Moriana waved back, and the warrior-woman was gone, Grutz lumbering after her.

Fost turned again to Moriana. He saw the peculiar light in her green eyes and thought with sinking heart of her scrying spell.

"Moriana . . ." he began.

She shook her head, placing a finger to his lips. "Don't worry," she said. She glanced at the trail. "I wish she'd said her name. She's quite a woman, isn't she?"

"Her name is Jennas," the courier said. "And yes, she is quite a woman indeed."

And so are you, he thought.

They trudged on during morning and afternoon. At first they walked strongly. Moriana, pausing to wait for Fost, had enjoyed several days of relative inactivity in which to recuperate from the endless trek south. Fost had gone through a more strenuous time but at least, as he told himself, he hadn't had to walk during most of it.

In a matter of only minutes, though, they were exhausted. The very clothes on their bodies weighted them down like the threat of impending death. Their feet were as hard to lift as if they had taken root. Step after dreary, dragging step all too slowly melted away the miles.

The day passed in leaden silence. After exhaustion stilled the happy conversation that had followed Moriana and Fost's reunion, even Erimenes soon lapsed into silence. He could not endure the empty, lonely way his voice rattled up and down the valleys walled with grey stone and mortared with ice.

The autumn polar day was short, and the sun no sooner gained the pinnacle of the sky than it tumbled to a bloody death on the jagged peaks. The onslaught of darkness brought with it redoubled chill. Fost and Moriana moved almost energetically as they erected Moriana's tent for the night. It was a counterfeit energy, born from their efforts to fight the weariness that urged them to lie on the bare, cold earth and sleep for all eternity.

Fingers half frozen, they found it hard even to wield spoons to spill a few mouthfuls of gruel down their throats. Bland as it was, the magical grey mess stung throats gone raw from breathing saw-edged antarctic air. At last they put away the ebony bowl and unrolled their bedrolls for sleep.

Fost wondered if it could have taken any more effort to climb the loftiest mountain in the Ramparts than it did to work his way down into the cocoon of his bed. Yet once he lay inside it, almost warm for the first time that day, he found sleep eluded him as nimbly as a handful of wind.

He lay a long time, becoming gradually more aware of the aches that assailed his body and of the breathing of the woman beside him. His mind was numb with fatigue, but he could not slip off the mantle of awareness. He realized Moriana's breathing did not come in the steady rhythm of sleep. He wondered what made her wakeful. She had to be as tired as he.

"Fost."

He rolled onto his back. He inhaled deliberately, thinking that his body would have stunk had not the cold leached odor from the air, or perhaps it was the sense of smell from his nostrils?

"Yes?"

"What happens once we get there?"

He breathed out. Vapor ghosted white above him. "Let's leave it," he said. His voice sounded ancient, a once-smooth baritone fractured by senescence. "We don't even know if we will get there."

"It's time we spoke of it," she insisted.

He shifted to his side. Her face was a pale blur in the darkness of the tent. His imagination filled in details: satin skin dried like leather by wind and sun, stretched taut over the frame of aristocratic cheekbones; full lips pressed tight, almost pinched, by the endless hours of forcing her body to go on, always on; her naturally bright eyes gone hard and sharp as emeralds; her golden hair turned to straw. Still, she was beautiful, as beautiful as only one can be whose spirit is strong, enduring and indomitable.

Fost freed his arm and reached out to stroke Moriana's cheek with the backs of his fingers. She turned her face away.

"You're evading the question," she accused. "I won't have it."

"What do you mean you won't have it?" he snapped, irritated by the tone of her voice.

She looked at him. He thought he could see the crystalline hardness in her eyes.

"There is a question that must be answered soon," Moriana said, the words sounding as if they'd been punched out with a cold chisel. "Who is to have the Amulet of Living Flame? We both desire it. Who gets it?"

Resentment geysered up inside Fost. He choked it back. Yet he knew it was this question, not the ache in his limbs, that kept sleep at a distance.

"I'm too sleepy to think straight," he said. "For Ust's sake, can't we talk about it tomorrow?" He shook his head. "Why can't we just *share* the damned amulet?"

"That's no answer," the princess hissed. Her hand shot from her roll and seized his wrist. Its grip reminded him of the grip of a Sky City eagle. "I want it to free my City. You want it for . . . carousal, so that you can drink and wench your way through the ages like some little boy who's just slipped over the edge into adolescence."

"To learn," Fost muttered. "I want to learn."

"There might only be limited power stored in the amulet. So it is written in the ancient scrolls Rann's men unearthed in Kolinth. So Erimenes affirms. If either of us uses it even once, it may turn into a useless trinket. *So who is to have it?*"

Fost twisted his hand from hers and rolled onto his back with a noisy exhalation.

Moriana reared up like an angry serpent. "You can't just turn away. Talk to me, dammit. I command it!"

"You *command* it?" Fost shot upright. "By what right do you command it?" His voice shook with outrage.

"By right of birth! I am Princess of the City in the Sky. I am *queen. That's* by what right, groundling."

"Queen? *Queen?* Of what? Of all the rocks and rodents in the Rampart Mountains?" He glared at her, nose hovering inches from hers.

For a long moment they stared at each other. Then Moriana said, "It looks that way, doesn't it?"

Fost blinked. Moriana snickered. She flopped onto her back and gave a hoot of laughter. His eyebrows rose. He tried to speak, but a laugh bubbled up from inside him and burst out past his words.

"I thought you were fighting." Erimenes's words cut astringently across their mirth. He sounded accusing.

"No, Erimenes," Fost gasped, trying to gulp in a lungful of air. "We're making love."

"If that's what you think you were doing, it explains why your companionship has been so markedly uninteresting of late. You could give lessons to a pair of mating felines."

Fost whooped and seized Moriana around the waist. Her fists pummeled his back, but not with the full strength she could put into them.

The courier's mind was clear with a kind of feverish lucidity as they grappled and groped their way toward an activity sure to alleviate the spirit's boredom. They had dissolved into laughter over nothing. Their mirth had been a release from the pressure building between them. In his curious acuteness of mind Fost recognized that for all her apparent determination on settling the question of the Amulet of Living Flame, Moriana had been no less eager than he to delay finding an answer.

Perhaps because there was no answer.

His hand slid into her bedroll, touched the yielding smoothness of bare skin. Her fingers kneaded the great muscle of his thigh. He groaned as his body responded despite the protests of overworked muscles.

Their bodies pressed against each other as if trying to blend into one. Yet the naked dagger of the unanswered question lay between them.

Fost felt a twinge in his back, so sharp he cried out. Moriana's mouth muffled the sound. The cramp faded and then she was on top of him.

CHAPTER
SEVEN

Prince Rann watched the snow fall.

The cold wind beat upon the sides of the makeshift pavilion. Tents had been hurriedly stitched together to form the shelter, lances and javelins comprising the uprights and the stark gray rock of the cliff forming the rear wall. It kept the survivors of his party reasonably dry. It seemed to hamper the cold not at all.

The prince shivered as icy tendrils of wind crept up his thigh. His right shoulder, bound tightly with linen, burned as hot as the brazier that provided the pavilion's sole heat. His side still ached from the love pat of Istu's Vicar, and his ribs seemed an ever-tightening band of iron around his chest. He tasted defeat and apprehension.

"Haven't you finished that spell yet?" he snapped at the scrawny youth who squatted near the brazier. The youth looked up, nervously running his fingers through his scraggly yellow beard.

"These things take time, lord," he whined. "Just now there is some disturbance in the ether. We aren't far from Athalau, center of magic inimical to ours."

"Don't lecture me, goat-whelp," the prince snapped. "Just finish your casting and be quick about it."

With a sniff the journeyman sorcerer turned back to the wide half geode propped on a bronze stand to present its polished face to him. Rann suppressed a snarl. Like political power, sorcerous ability passed mostly along the feminine side of the Etuul clan. Rann had some spells, but numbered neither scrying nor the use of the seeing-stone among them. So he must abide with the sorcerer's impudence if he wished to communicate with the Sky City. He viewed the prospect with a feeling as near dread as he was capable of, but call he must.

He thought of how satisfying it would be to flay the impudent sorcerer. The very notion twisted his nerves and gave him stirrings in useless loins. But he couldn't punish the journeyman mage—he was needed. He must not punish those fools who had let the bear-riders take his elite Sky Guardsmen in the rear and rob him of his vengeance upon Fost Longstrider. If he wished, he could return to the Great Crater Lake and torment a few Ethereals, but they met their sufferings with bland indifference. He might as well be inflicting torment on a brass statue for all the satisfaction it would give him. Tension built unbearably in him, tension of the sort he had ever been wont to ease through the suffering of others. Now it found no outlet.

As they had been erecting this rough shelter against the buffeting winds, a creature had darted from its burrow beneath their boots. Quick as a serpent he had snatched up the small furry thing and snapped its neck with a convulsion of his hands. The killing had given him momentary satisfaction, but only momentary. The death had been too quick, too painless. It offered nothing of catharsis.

Now he sat twining his fingers together with a force that threatened to snap their joints. He prepared himself for abasement before his cousin, for he had failure to report and assistance to beg. It was almost enough to make him start to scream and never stop.

"Lord Prince," the youthful mage said obsequiously through his snout. "Our Most Gracious Majesty, Queen Synalon, awaits your pleasure."

Squinting at the youth in disgust, Rann entertained the thought of seizing him by the scruff of the neck and thrusting his face into the coals. Perhaps he could sear off a few of the pimples scattered like pustulant rubies across his visage. He shook himself and moved to stand in front of the geode.

Its surface glowed with the likeness of Synalon. She lolled on her jeweled throne, fingers idly stroking the feathers of a large raven. Her scarlet gown opened to the navel, baring slices of creamy breast. Rann's tongue danced across his lips. She smiled, knowing the consternation it caused him to see her thus.

"Well, cousin," she purred, "we trust you've only triumph to report?"

The very silkiness of her tone indicated that she trusted no such thing. Rann swallowed hard.

"I regret, O Mistress of the Clouds, that my expedition has met with a temporary setback."

Synalon nodded, her eyes half closed.

The prince cleared his throat. "I would not trouble Your Majesty, save that I must request you release to me more troops."

"More troops?" She arched a brow. "What exigencies might you encounter that a half-company of our finest Guardsmen are insufficient to deal with?"

Rann swallowed gall. "None, Sky-born," he said, "yet I no longer possess half a company. Only twelve men remain, twelve out of fifty."

"How is this?" Tersely Rann told her of their losses to storm, thulyakhashawin and finally to the bear-riding nomads. "It distresses us that a handful of barbarians could slaughter our elite with such ease." She plucked a morsel from a bowl at her elbow and offered it to the raven. The bird gobbled it down, regarding Rann with an unwinking crimson bead of an eye.

Rann fought down a grimace. Her affectation of the royal "we" irritated him, and he despised her poison-taloned pets.

"They came upon us from behind, Majesty."

"Indeed." Her hand ruffled the feathers behind the

raven's head. "The foremost of our chieftains permits himself to be taken in the rear by a passel of savages. Is this the man we trust to bring us victory?"

"My life is yours," the prince said. He bowed his head.

"You'll not get off that easily," Synalon sneered. Rann looked up in alarm. "It is your fate to serve the Throne of the City. Though we need them for our own preparations, we will release to you another fifty Sky Guardsmen." She stroked the bird's beak. It croaked delight at the attention. "See that you do not disappoint us again. Bring us the amulet—*and my sister!*"

"Your Majesty," he almost gasped. "I assure you . . ." With a wave of her hand, Synalon broke the connection as the words left her cousin's mouth. He sat back, boiling with rage as sweat streamed down his face.

The journeyman magician sat by with folded hands and an unctuous expression. "Does my lord require anything else?"

"Yes," Rann snapped. "The stink of the latrine trench begins to affront my nostrils. Do something about it, Maguerr, or I'll bury you to the neck in it so that you may fully appreciate the savor of the sewage."

He smiled at the boy's expression of horror. It made him feel somewhat better.

The travelers had tramped so long through a fog compounded of tedium, exhaustion and bone-stabbing cold that it took them some minutes to realize they had come to the other side of the mountains.

The storm had gone its way. The swollen sun squeezed into the eastern sky, turning the far mountains to copper. At the faint caress of winter sunlight on her cheeks, Moriana raised her head.

"Ooooh!" A long syllable of wonder rolled from her

lips. She clutched at her companion's arm. "Fost, look. Look!"

He lifted his head and blinked. Weak as the morning sun was, it dazzled him after the long night. Tinged with pink, the icefields stretched away forever southward: the Southern Waste. And that meant to the east lay . . .

He swiveled his head toward the sunrise.

Moriana turned with him, and her gasp rose with his. High mountains formed a bowl beyond which stretched the Gulf of Veluz like a sheet of beaten bronze. In their amazement they took no note of the distant water. A nearer spectacle claimed their eyes.

The glacier filled the bowl between the mountains. It was no blank whiteness like the icelands beyond but was an enormous swirl of bands of color, dark on light. Brown, white, black, yellow, dull red and green cast back flecks of sunlight here and there so that the whole sparkled and danced in the sun. It reminded Fost of candles he'd seen with different hues of wax poured together in colorful whorls.

"Is that the glacier?" Moriana asked breathlessly. "I thought it would be dull and white."

Erimenes answered her. "It is indeed a glacier, my dear. Its progress scoops up earth and rock from the ground below, which accounts for the bands of differing shade. Additionally other, lesser glaciers flow into it from the surrounding mountains, causing the most remarkable patterns. Observe."

"Enough," Fost growled. His heart had begun to hammer his ribs in excitement. Then his gorge rose at a horrible thought. He ripped Erimenes's jug from his satchel and shook it violently.

"Come out of there, you poor excuse for a ghost," he shrieked. When he unstoppered the bottle, blue mist flowed forth. The fog became a miniature tornado with dancing light-motes like the sparkles out on the ice. But Erimenes was a little bluer than usual, from motion sickness.

"Wh-what's the matter?" asked Moriana, confused at Fost's behavior.

"The city—the force of the glacier must have pulverized it to dust. We've come all this way for nothing!" Fost raised his arm to smash the jug.

"Wait!" cried Erimenes. His spectral arm swept out from his side. "Behold," he said.

One broad band near the center of the bowl glowed pale blue. It was to this the spirit pointed. Fost squinted. He realized the ice was not tinted but lay clear, its blue the blue of the cloudless sky above. *Is it my imagination?* he wondered, *or do I glimpse shapes within, spires and minarets and bulging domes?*

"Behold Athalau," Erimenes said with pride. "Behold my home. The magic of Athalau has not diminished. The glacier is hollow inside."

The ice-locked shapes showed clearer now. The structures of that fragment of Athalau they could see had an airy, almost fragile look, similiar to that within the City in the Sky, but without its subtle and disturbing distortion. Yet it must be monumentally strong to have withstood the pressure of countless tons of ice across the years. His respect for the power of the city's builders grew as he stood looking on a tableau literally frozen for eternity.

His limbs began to quiver. Adrenaline excitement buzzed in his ears, and his veins sang impatiently.

"Erimenes! How do we get in?" Weariness fell from him like a dropped cloak.

"Do be patient," the sage said, turning an airy smirk in his direction. "I've gone fourteen hundred years not knowing how I might once again return to my home. You can wait a while longer."

"Untrue!" Fost shouted. "Merely thirteen hundred ninety-nine. And besides, I know I'll have to wait to enter Athalau—we're a good day's travel away. What I'm asking is, how will we get in once we're there?"

"Now, now." Erimenes wagged a finger. "You must trust me."

"*Trust* you?" Fost bellowed. "I'd sooner trust a starving wolf."

The spirit looked hurt. "After all I've done for you," he sighed, "such ingratitude is wormwood indeed. Well then, if we're going to fall to mistrusting one another, how can I trust you? How do I know that, once I impart my knowledge to you, you won't abandon me here to sit alone throughout eternity with no companion save the howling wind?"

"He's right," Moriana said. "We can wait to learn how he plans to gain entry to the glacier. He would hardly have brought us this far without knowing how. We have to trust him."

She didn't add, *as we have to trust each other*. He eyed her measuringly and saw the same calculation in her eyes. She was hearing the call of the Amulet of Living Flame as keenly as he. The reckoning could not long be forestalled. A shadow crossed the day.

She leaned forward, rising on her toes to kiss his lips. "We've almost made it," she said. "Against all odds, we're almost there. They'll sing of us, Fost. The bards will commemorate us for generations."

The problem of gaining entry to the city in the glacier still worried him, and to his mind no empty strophes sung by weak-wristed poets could match centuries of brawling, lusty life. He couldn't rid himself of the certainty that she intended to have the former rather than the latter. But he shrugged his doubts aside and returned her kiss boldly. Then arm in arm they started down the mountainside.

Nightfall found them within a few miles of the glacier's edge. As a parting gift Jennas had given Fost a pack filled with supplies. From this they took a tent and a bit of firewood, more priceless than jewels in the treeless waste. Fost and Moriana dined on a haunch of meat they found in the pack. When the fire died down, they climbed into a bedroll to share the warmth of their bodies. Their lovemaking was still more fervent than that which, the night before, had marked their reunion. Tomorrow they would enter Athalau—providing Erimenes knew the way in. Tomorrow, or soon after, they would possess the Amulet of Living Flame. And then must be answered the question of who should have it.

So their bodies writhed together with restless urgency, knotting, spasming, resting limp with repletion and then building eagerness, thrusting and receiving, until their strength was gone and they slept, undreaming, too tired to brood that this time might have been their last.

Fost had to tilt his head far back to see the top of the blue ice wall. It hadn't occurred to him it would rise so high. The chill seemed to beat from it in waves.

He turned away to hunker by the fire Moriana had built at the glacier's foot. She toasted the last remnants of their meat on Fost's metal spit. Excited, they had risen with the sun and marched on without breaking fast. Within three hours they had reached the farthest extent of the glacier-swallowing sheet of ice. Now was time for resting, eating and taking counsel.

Moriana passed him a sizzling scrap. He wolfed it down, relishing the meaty flavor and letting the juices roll down his throat. Nearby swayed the figure of Erimenes, beaming down on the pair like a mother hen. Fost looked at him.

"Well, old spirit," he said expansively. "The time, as the wise are wont to say, has come. Tell us how to get inside the city."

"All you need do is ask," the spirit said.

"I am asking." Fost's face clouded.

"No, no," Erimenes said. "Ask the glacier."

Fost's head snapped around. He eyed the nebulous visage for signs of levity. "Ask the . . . glacier?"

Erimenes nodded.

"Treachery!" roared Fost, leaping to his feet. He shook his fist under Erimenes's nose. "I knew it! I knew this vaporous scoundrel lied when he said he'd get us in!" He swept a burning red brand from the fire and hurled it against the ice.

"Ouch," said a voice.

Fost turned around. The word rolled past him like a boulder and went booming off across the flats. He eyed his companions. Moriana's face showed surprise and Erimenes's no more than its usual quota of smug superiority.

"Is this a trick of yours, Erimenes?"

"It's rather late in my life for my voice to deepen so," the spirit said. "Likewise, I deem it unlikely the luscious Moriana has been magically transformed into a basso profundo."

"If you didn't speak, who did?"

"I did." The words came louder than before, striking Fost like a sea wave. He turned toward the cliff of ice, seeking their origin. Superstitious fear prickled his neck-hairs. His sword came into his hand.

"Who is 'I'?" he demanded.

A heavy sigh swept over him. "Too long has it been since I discoursed with humans," the voice said. The words fell slowly, like water dripping from the tip of an icicle. Fost felt an urge to prod the speaker to greater speed, but as yet he had no idea who the speaker was. "I don't seem to recall them as being so blind that they cannot see something before their very eyes. Are you as the heat-hunters, then, humans?"

Erimenes tittered. Fost shot him a poisoned look which hardly stilled the spirit.

"O great-voiced one," the courier said, "forgive my slowness. Only please tell me who and where you are."

"Can you really not see me? If you stretch out your hand you'll touch me. At the point where your party lies, my flank is over a hundred feet high, though I'm far thicker in places."

Comprehension slowly dawned. "You mean . . . you're the *glacier?*" Fost stared.

"Of course," the voice said.

Fost felt Moriana come up beside him. Her arm encircled his waist. She snuggled against him for warmth, looking up at the glacier with round eyes.

"You devoured Athalau," she said.

A groan came from the depths of the ice. "Not my doing, not my doing," the glacier said ponderously. "I go where the slow pull of the planet drags me, where the pressure of falling snow drives me. Athalau was a fair city; fair were its folk and wise above all others."

The glacier sighed again. The sheer ice wall shuddered. A few hundred yards to the wayfarers' right, a chunk of ice broke from the clifftop and came crashing down. Fost and Moriana jumped back, gazing anxiously up the glacier's side.

The glacier did not notice. "Fair were the Athalar, and foul were the Hissing Ones, and so they waged war. Long they fought the reptiles, and mightily. For all their wisdom the Athalar could not defeat the power of Istu, Demon of the Dark Ones. Not till the Blessed

Felarod with his Hundred summoned up the Earth-Spirit did the light prevail. Great things transpired in that War of Powers. Continents sank, a star fell out of heaven, the very Earth tipped on its axis so the ice crept north to cover Athalau." Its voice was sad. "The raw power of the Earth-Spirit infused many things—the rocks, the mountains, the very snow. Thus did I come to life. But not to power over my own destiny. No. All willy-nilly I moved onward. Though it tore at my heart, I overran Athalau. It lies entombed within me."

The recitation took fifteen minutes and was filled with many a dolorous pause. Fost sat on a large rock and drew Moriana close. When at last the glacier finished, he asked, "Can you make a path for us to Athalau? We have journeyed long and faced much to reach the city. But if you cannot control your, uh, body, we may have come this way for nothing."

"I can control what my body does within itself, though, I fear, not well," the glacier answered ponderously. "But, know you: To atone for the wrong I unwillingly did the Athalar, I made with them a compact. I am to guard Athalau until the end of time, to keep the Fallen People or other agents of the Dark Ones from misusing the mighty secrets locked inside to spread their terror across the globe. You appear harmless enough, and your eyes are poor. But how do I know you are what you claim to be?"

"Do hurry and get this over with," called Erimeñes. "It makes me cold just looking at this lump of ice."

The glacier rumbled.

"Don't mind my spiritualistic friend," Fost said hurriedly. "He tends to babble. But he is himself an Athalar by birth. You may have heard of him. Erimenes the Ethical."

"Oromanes," the glacier mused. "No, the name is unfamiliar."

"Erimenes," the spirit said. "I was, dare I say it, the last great sage of Athalau. I taught that the material world and all its trappings are but illusion and to be spurned."

"Ah, yes," the glacier said. "I do recall you, Arrimines. Some of your pupils used to come and try to convert me to their views. I found them foolish. I am real. The snow that feeds me, the earth below my belly, the sun that burns fat from my back in the springtime, all these are real."

Erimenes made a mournful sound. "You are wise," he said. "Would that I had been as well. I grew more and more otherworldly as my life wore on. Then, when my body died, I barely noticed, so tenuous had my connections with it become. My spirit lived on. After my physical death, when it was far too late, I realized how wrong I'd been. The world of sensation is like a treasure trove and must be cherished. The path of true wisdom is the pursuit of pleasure."

"An equally callow view. I have had one hundred centuries to mull, and the middle path seems best to me. I flow between mountains, trying to climb neither one nor the other."

"Bah. Moderation should be enjoyed in moderation. Life should be lived to the fullest. Each instant should pulse with hot sensation, each beat of the heart should be quick with passion, each . . ."

"No one cares, Erimenes," Moriana said. "Tell me, glacier, have you a name?"

The glacier pondered a mere ten minutes. " 'Guardian' will serve, I think. I guard sacred Athalau and its secrets."

"Very well, Guardian. A former inhabitant of Athalau has returned to his home after long years of separation. Will you let us in?"

"Home." Shifting sounds came from inside the

glacier. "Often have I wished I could share the comfort you warm ones take from the concept, yet to me it means nothing. No place is my home; I cannot leave where I am. I grow by traveling. Though, did the earth resume its earlier inclination and the sun drive me back south, I would miss the caress of these mountains. Many lesser glaciers have formed within them and flowed to meet me, and so become part of me. Ah, the diversity of feeling I have learned to love! Perhaps you feel so about *home*."

The humans sat as the words emerged with painful slowness. They understood the glacier's deliberation; what need had it to hurry? But its speech dragged on endlessly till they found themselves nodding and blinking despite the cold and their impatience to reach Athalau. When at last the slow word flow stopped, Moriana nudged Fost in the ribs, breaking off a loud snore.

"Will you let us in?" she asked again.

"I have agreed to let no nonresidents into the city," the glacier said, "but nothing was said about those who accompanied an Athalar."

"Erimenes is confined to his jug," Moriana said, "and cannot reach Athalau without us to carry him. And know that in my veins flows the blood of Athalau." She avoided mentioning that she traced her lineage through the City in the Sky. The two cities had often warred between the downfall of the Fallen Ones and the onset of the ice.

"Ahhhh," the glacier said. It fell silent in thought.

Fost sat, chin sunk in hand. Moriana paced. Erimenes allowed a gentle breeze to push his vaporous substance into a spiral.

"I'm freezing," Moriana said finally. "How long will it take the glacier to decide?"

"Not long, I shouldn't think," Erimenes said lightly.

"Not long? What's long to a glacier?"

"Perhaps there's another way in," said Fost.

"Don't even think such thoughts," Erimenes said, gesticulating nervously. "The glacier will never admit us if we anger him, as trying to break into Athalau would surely do. Besides, an army could dig for a generation without reaching the city. And once inside, it could be crushed by a mere shrug!" The misty shape hugged itself and shivered. "To be immured in ice forever, barred from all sensation but undying cold—*brrr!*"

"You can't feel the cold, Erimenes," Moriana pointed out. "Besides, your lot would still be no worse than that of anyone else who's dead."

"I don't care about them," the spirit said waspishly. "Though I've no body, to be surrounded for millennia with walls of ice would make me *think* I was cold. It's only psychology."

"Great Ultimate protect us from it, if it can make the dead suffer," Fost said. "Is that how the demons of hell torment their victims, by using this psychology? Ust knows you're the only dead man I've ever known to whom it made a bit of difference what anyone did to him. I've found the dead an apathetic lot, by and large."

Erimenes threw up his hands at Fost's lack of perception. The courier huddled deeper into his bearskin and grumbled, "You might be able to feel the cold at that. The damned wind stabs through me like a spear. I wish we had enough wood to make a real fire."

"We'd have to move away if we did," said Moriana. "We don't want to make Guardian uncomfortable."

"I know," piped up Erimenes. "I have a wonderful way you two can keep warm. Cast away your bulky garments and fornicate. The heat of passion and exercise will warm you better than any cloak!"

Moriana didn't deign to answer. She sat down beside

Fost and leaned against him. His arm went naturally around her shoulders.

They were sound asleep when two hours later the glacier's answer rumbled forth. "I do not like to make snap decisions," Guardian said, "but I understand the impetuousness of your kind. You seem goodly folk to me, and the arguments in favor of allowing Uromines . . ."

"Erimenes!" the spirit corrected sharply.

". . . into the city are most persuasive. That Erimanus is a ghost is not to be held against him; Athalau is now a ghost city as well." The voice stopped, waiting expectantly. "Ah, well. A joke, but no matter. As I was saying, it seems unjust to deny an Athalar entrance to his native city, and since he requires the aid of his companions to reach the city, I must admit them too. Admittedly the young lady's lineage, deriving as it does from Athalau, was a factor in my deciding. However . . ."

Fost found himself leaning perilously far forward, straining for the glacier's next word. He wanted to beat his fists against the ice to force words from it. Guardian had decided to let them into Athalau, but what were its conditions? The promise of eternal life filled him with wild energy.

Just when he thought he'd go mad if he must wait a second more, the glacier spoke again. "However, in return for admitting you, I ask a boon."

"Anything!" Fost shouted. Moriana echoed him.

"I am infested with worms. The pesky things burrow about within me, wiggling and twitching and causing me endless misery."

Fost frowned. Anything that could cause serious discomfort to something as immense as the glacier was something he would think twice about blithely promising to put an end to.

"It will be dark in a matter of hours," Erimenes pointed out. "Do the crusty old ice cube a favor and go after the ice-worms for him so we don't have to spend the night in this abominable wind."

"We'll do what we can, Guardian," Moriana said.

"Very well, then," the glacier said. "Enter."

The ice mountain shook. Clutching each other, Fost and Moriana fell against the cliff. At any moment they expected tons of ice and snow to smash down on them from above.

Instead the ice gave with a tremendous groan and split with a cracking like a million thunderbolts. Debris rained down, but nothing struck the travelers but wet clumps of snow.

"Enter," Guardian said again. "But be quick. I cannot hold the way open for long."

Fost and Moriana grabbed their packs, recapping Erimenes's jar and stuffing it into the satchel. Slipping, they ran into the crevice. It was about as wide as Fost was tall. An upward glance told him it didn't reach more than fifty feet up the cliff face.

Eerie, glistening dark surrounded them. They moved as rapidly as they could into the glacier, keeping arms outstretched to keep themselves upright. The ice underfoot was incredibly slick.

"We need to get out of this damned crack," Fost said, then clamped his mouth shut as his own voice exploded in his ears, trapped by walls of ice. More quietly he went on, "We'll never find a way without light. I wonder if it's safe to light a torch?"

"Guardian," Moriana called, wincing at the loudness of her voice. "Can we light a torch here inside you? We must have light to see."

"If you must, you must." The glacier spoke with unwonted haste. The strain of holding open the crack ran like a taut thread through its words. Razor-sharp shards of ice fell from the ceiling, and Fost thought the walls lurched inwards an inch. "But hurry! I can't . . . keep . . . this up . . . much longer."

Moriana dug in the pack. She found two splinters of pine and thrust them toward the courier. His groping fingers found them in the blackness. From his own pack he drew flint and steel and a tinder-bowl. Here in the bowels of the glacier the air was moist and not good for fire-making. Fumbling with haste, it took Fost several tries to get a spark into the tinder. One fell into the dry lichen, glowed, waned. He blew frantically.

With a small sizzling noise, a flame flared up. Hastily Fost lit the splinters. The resinous wood caught eagerly and burned with a smoky yellow light. The ice walls of the crack threw back the light in eye-stabbing golden spears. Fost blinked away the glare and the party hurried on.

A moan came from the bouncing satchel. "Oh, make haste, make haste!" Erimenes cried. "I can feel Guardian weakening. The walls will crush us at any moment, and I shall be entombed in ice forever. Woe!"

"Your home city is ice-entombed, so it's not unfitting you should be too." Fost panted the words, short of breath from the effort of running along the slick, uneven surface. Despite his flip response he was no less worried than the spirit. He felt the trembling in the walls, as if their muscles were overtired and failing fast.

A sharp report rolled through the crevice. The ice walls shifted. Moriana screamed as they touched her shoulders.

Running ahead of her, Fost gasped as the hardness pressed in on both sides. His shoulders were forced inward, his arms beginning to pop from their sockets. Erimenes keened despair.

The glacier groaned. The walls slid back, though not as far as they'd been before.

"Time is short," Guardian groaned. The words boomed out around Fost and Moriana, who felt as though they scurried along the inside of a giant drum while it was being beaten by a drummer. "The next time the walls slip, I can help . . . you . . . no . . . moooore!"

Fost pounded his hand against Erimenes's satchel. In his own frenzy of fear and desperation he could not bear the spirit's wailing. *Is this how it ends?* he thought frantically. *So near to eternal life, to have life crushed from me? I see no end to this crevice. How can we get out before the walls close in?* Claustrophobic fingers clutched at his throat. *O Ust, how can we escape?*

Moriana seized his arm. "There," she shouted. "Up ahead—to the left!" The dark gleam of ice was interrupted by a patch of blackness perfectly round and wider than Fost was tall. Fost put on a burst of speed, racing with Moriana at his side. Halfway, his feet slipped. His legs pumped harder and the last ten yards were crossed in a sort of running fall. He reached the tunnel, twisted to the side and dived in, sliding thirty feet on his belly. Something soft bumped his bootsoles. He turned.

"Moriana!"

The princess nodded, brushing back blond hair. Behind her the crack slammed shut with a sound that made their insides quiver.

Moriana and Fost crawled toward each other, reached and clung like babies, shaking with reaction. Had it not been for the tunnel, they would have been pulverized more thoroughly than any denizen of the Valley of Crushed Bones.

The same thought struck both at once. *Why* was the tunnel here? And why hadn't it closed as well?

"I shouldn't tarry here, if I were you two." The terror was gone from Erimenes's voice, and his usual truculence had taken its place. "This tunnel was made by the ice-worms, if you haven't guessed, and that's why it hasn't been closed off. If the Guardian could shut them, he would have put an end to the worms long since." The spirit paused. "The worms are attracted to vibrations, you know. Best move along lest they put an end to you."

The pair struggled to their feet. Swords swished into their hands. Fost still wore the long mail vest the bear-folk had given him; he had left behind the helmet and shield, which, while useful, were too burdensome to carry. It seemed pathetically little with which to defend against such beings as his imagination made the worms.

"Erimenes," he said softly, hoping the vibrations of his voice wouldn't carry to any questing monsters. "Can you get your bearings? Can you sense how we should proceed?"

"Naturally. If you fare along this tunnel, in a few hundred yards you'll come to a cross-tunnel that should bring you to the outskirts of Athalau. Ah, to see my home again!"

Sounds came through the ice as Fost and Moriana paced along the icy passage. Some were readily identifiable as the sounds of the glacier, settlings and rumblings and deep shifting. Others they couldn't recognize: sounds that had a furtive tone that made the two uneasy. Fost wondered if Erimenes had lied about being able to sense where they were and how to reach the city from there. If he told the truth, it was further evidence that the shade possessed formidable powers. Who knew what he might be able to do as he came even nearer to the city of his birth?

"Erimenes," Moriana asked, "is it wise to burn these torches? Won't they eat our air?"

"Tut, tut, my dear, fear not. The ice-worm tunnels have thoroughly honeycombed our friend the

Guardian; little wonder he's so annoyed. Some of their tunnels reach the surface. The beasts feed on other dwellers in the glacier and sometimes on each other. But at times they venture out at night to feed on the ice."

"At night?"

"They loathe the light. Even the antarctic sun, feeble as it is, suffices to kill them."

The tunnel twisted ahead of them. The two tried to go as quietly as they could, but it proved difficult. Footfalls slap-slap-slapped away from them, seeming to grow in volume as they preceded the travelers. When Moriana tried running her feet along the ice without lifting them, the rasping sound was nearly as loud. They just had to run lightly and fast—and pray.

"Just a few yards more, my children," Erimenes told them. "Around this next bend is the crossway I told you about. So I regret to inform you . . ."

Fost rounded the bend and dug in his heels. The ice failed to give purchase. He slid forward, pinwheeling his arms, and fell onto his rump.

". . . there are the worms," Erimenes finished unnecessarily.

Scrambling, Fost got to his feet. Moriana stood beside him, her sword a crimson arc in the torchlight. Twenty feet away the ice-worms waited.

Like greatly magnified earthworms, but the color of snow, their segmented bodies tapered to blunt ends, and these were tipped with hard-looking black caps. A knot of them filled the passageway, writhing together so that the horrified pair couldn't tell how many they faced. The creatures came in assorted sizes, from one a foot thick to a giant better than four feet through the middle. How long the things might be neither Fost nor Moriana could guess.

The largest worm moved forward, crowding aside its

lesser fellows. Short, stiff cilia in its rear segments gripped the ice while its forepart squeezed toward them, elongating. The travelers drew back, swords warily extended. The monster's anterior segments widened, the bristles bit and it drew its body forward with a gruesome slithering.

The head rose, blind and questing. The black cap opened like a flower. The shiny surface split into four even wedges like pieces of a pie and opened to reveal a broad, slimy throat. Inside were toothed sphincters that pulsated even as the humans watched.

They loathe the light went through Fost's brain. He thrust his torch before him like a rapier and lunged. Hissing, the worm drew back.

"Ha!" the courier shouted. "These worms are not so much. See how it fears the flame? Into the tunnel, Moriana." Advancing a step at a time, he drove the giant worm back far enough that the princess could slip by and into the side passage. Behind the great worm others thrashed in rage, slamming their heads against the walls and hissing angrily.

"There," said Fost smugly. "Nothing to it."

The ice-worm lunged.

Fost threw himself backward. The vast mouth encircled the torch and the jaws slammed together. The tunnel plunged into absolute darkness.

Fost fell again, propelling himself backward with his legs. He felt rather than saw the bulk of the worm coming after him.

"Erimenes, you treacherous blue fart! You said they hated the light, said it could kill them!"

His eyes accustomed themselves to the gloom. From the side passage Moriana's torch cast a feeble glow. It illuminated the head of the worm, striking this way and that in blind agony.

"Sunlight can kill them," the spirit's voice floated

out. "They hate light of any sort, but torchlight poses no danger to them. Athalar scientists long theorized that some component found in sunlight but missing from torchlight is what kills them. And, as has just been amply demonstrated, sufficiently keen hunger can overcome their aversion to light weaker than that of the sun."

"I don't want a lecture. How do I kill the damned things?"

"That," said the philosopher primly, "is rather your problem, is it not?"

Distracted, Fost missed the creature's quick, purposeful movement. It had recovered from the frenzy of pain the torch had caused it. Nearly too late, Fost snatched back his hand as the head darted forward. Chitinous jaws clacked shut an inch from his fingertips.

He jabbed with his sword, felt it bite. The head jerked back with a hiss of annoyance. The worm's breath smelled like a mouldering corpse. Fost heard a sound like an axe chopping wood. The head reared back, giving off a thin, whistling scream.

"I'll help you, Fost," he heard Moriana call. "I'm attacking the thing. Great Ultimate, but it's slimy!"

Her sword struck again. The worm keened and went for Fost. He hacked, his blade bouncing off a mandible. The head pulled back, swaying. Moriana's blows fell with a regular rhythm, but the worm ignored her now, keeping its attention firmly on the courier. He was on his feet again, crouched low, dagger in one hand and his sword in the other. He tried to match the unpredictable movements of the ghastly head, but the thing was quick. Again and again the worm's head snapped forward. Fost met it as best he could with parries.

The worm shot forward, lurching over the defense of his dagger. The quartet of jaws gouged his left bicep even as the dagger sank into wormflesh. He thrust his sword deep into the fourth ring-segment. The worm withdrew. His blade slipped free covered with foul yellow slime.

"Fost! I've done it!" Moriana cried in triumph. "I've cut the thing in two!"

"Many thanks, Princess," he called. Thinking his enemy slain, he started forward.

The worm's head slammed into his breast. The jaws closed with a crunching sound. Mail rings snapped like spun sugar, and Fost gasped as muscles tore. He cut wildly at the gleaming segments, dropping his dagger to push at the rubbery, slick hide.

"Gormanka, won't anything kill this thing?" A frantic wrench freed him. He fell back, feeling his blood gush from the wound in his chest.

"Merely dissecting it will most assuredly not do so," Erimenes said. "You must strike the brain to kill it."

Not seeming to miss its latter half, the worm hunched forward, stalking Fost. It had the taste of his blood now. It hungered for more.

"Where *is* its brain?" Fost shouted.

"In the head, naturally. On top, within the fourth and fifth ring-segments. Can't miss it." The philosopher indulged in a chuckle. "At least, you'd *better* not. . . ."

Fost heard the other worms feasting on the large one's tail. The flesh tore with a blubbering sound that sickened him. He wondered how his own would sound as the black jaws rent it.

With sudden inspiration he reversed his grip on the sword. The basket made it hard to hold point-downward. He met the worm's sallies with jabs, goading it to fury. It was too quick for him to sink a killing thrust, but he lacerated the flesh around its mouth until the head was smeared with ichor.

At last, frustrated in its attempts to reach the man-thing with its crushing jaws by rearing, the worm dropped its head low and struck serpentlike along the floor. It was what Fost had been awaiting. As it struck he dived, flinging his legs out behind him and stabbing down. The sword point struck between the fourth and fifth segments and sank deep.

The worm's death-throes slammed Fost against the roof of the tunnel. He hung on grimly, but the spasms were too violent and tore loose his hold on the sword. Dashed to the floor, he lay there feeling like a giant bruise until the thing was still.

His hilt protruded from the monster's neck. Its struggles had driven the sword full-length into it so that Fost had to pull with both hands to free the weapon. Then he stood back taking stock of the situation.

The bulk of the dead worm lay between Fost and its fellows, leaving no room to pass. It also lay between Fost and Moriana. He frowned, absently wiping blood and worm gore from his chest.

"Well done, Fost," congratulated Erimenes.

"You didn't seem any too concerned, spirit in a jug. Did the prospect of riding about in a worm's gut not upset you?" Fost asked.

"Oh, I was confident of Moriana's overcoming the brute, even if you failed." Erimenes sounded cheerful. "Besides, I might have been able to make i—" He bit off the sentence abruptly.

"Make it what?" Fost asked, suspicions blooming within him.

"Make it, uh, well, you see—make it into an enlightening experience?" A rising note made the sentence into a question. Fost shook his head. The spirit was lying, and he didn't like what that implied.

He opened his mouth. Moriana's cry overrode his question.

"Fost! Hurry! The worms are eating their way through the dead one's tail."

Cursing that he had no time to pursue the matter with Erimenes, Fost cast about for a way of reaching the side tunnel. The worm had drawn its forepart up to anchor itself for the fight with Fost, which meant its segments had spread out to fill most of the tunnel. He couldn't get by on the sides and there wasn't sufficient room to squeeze along its top. The grisly sounds of feasting grew nearer.

"If I may make a suggestion?" Erimenes asked hesitantly. Fost stared at him. "The ice-worms, like their earth-delving cousins, consist largely of a tube within a tube. This one's alimentary passage, as I'm sure you noted, is more than sufficient to accommodate your girth."

"Are you suggesting . . . ?" Fost swallowed heavily as he eyed the body of the worm.

"Do you see any other way?"

Moriana called again for him to hurry. He chewed the inside of his cheek. Nausea and horror squirmed to knot in his belly at what Erimenes proposed, but he could see no alternative. He sheathed his sword, unslung the satchel and dropped to his knees. Taking a deep breath, he forced open the ice-worm's jaws and crawled in.

Blackness and stink assailed his senses. The teeth rimming the large sphincters tore at his flesh where it was exposed. He shut his eyes, mouth and nose and began to wiggle forward, glad he didn't have to see where he was going.

The oozing walls of the intestine closed in around him, caressing him with a touch unsettlingly like that of the tentacled, human-faced guardian of Kleta-atelk's cliff. His mouth filled with sour vomit. He made himself swallow it and moved on.

Digestive acids stung his flesh. The open cuts on his arms and chest felt as though coals had been dropped into them. His face stung. Ropes of mucus trailed over his lips and nose and tangled in his hair. He felt madness rising within him. *I'm trapped in here,* he thought irrationally. *Trapped forever in the stench and the filth and the clamminess and the darkness, gods, the darkness. . . .*

His hand probed ahead of him and found cool air. Then the other, dragging Erimenes's satchel, broke free of the worm's gut. Finally his head emerged, dripping and fetuslike into the glare of Moriana's torch. The princess dropped to her knees with a glad cry, leaned forward to kiss him. She stopped abruptly.

He shook his head. Droplets of milky digestive fluid flew. He carefully rubbed his eyes clear of it before opening them.

"Fost, I'm so glad you made it," said Moriana.

He marked how she kept her head held away and smiled. "If you're so pleased, how about a welcoming kiss?"

She blanched. He laughed, wiggling from the disgusting cocoon of the worm's belly, and stood.

"You can owe it to me," he said.

"They're after us," Fost said, ear pressed to the wall of the tunnel.

"I could have told you that," Erimenes informed him loftily.

Fost shook his head. "I'm none too sure how far to trust you."

"That again!" Erimenes's voice quavered with outrage. "I warned you of the worms before, did I not?"

"For reasons of your own," Moriana said. "I wonder if they are ours. You sold me to Synalon readily enough. What do you call that, if not treachery?"

"Expedience. It's all in the point of view."

As they talked, Fost and Moriana jogged along the

sinuous tunnel. The spirit informed them they were drawing steadily nearer to the limits of Athalau. They didn't know how much stock to put in his words.

"I've helped you both again and again," Erimenes said. "I've saved your lives—both of them—on many occasions the last few weeks. Admit it!"

Moriana exchanged a glance with Fost. "You have," she said grudgingly. "But somehow your solicitousness troubles me more than your earlier eagerness to involve everybody around you in wholesale slaughter."

Erimenes sniffed. The fleeing pair passed another tunnel entryway. Many passages crossed the one they followed. Erimenes had counseled them to ignore these. The tunnel they were in would bring them to where they wished to be.

"Fost?" Erimenes asked.

"Pipe down, you noisome old bottle of wind." The courier had had enough of the spirit's weasel-words for now.

Then he and Moriana rounded a new bend. The worms were waiting. The huge slimy creatures shrank away from the light.

"How did they get in front of us?" Moriana asked. "You said this was the straightest route!"

"So I did, child. But you aren't thinking clearly. These are not at all the same worms you encountered before. It's an entirely new . . . pack? Flock? Dear me, what *is* the proper collective for ice-worms?"

"Why didn't you warn us?" demanded Fost, drawing his sword.

"I tried to. I was told to pipe down," the spirit said. "Ahem. A wiggle of worms? No, no, that's still not right. Incidentally you'd best make short work of these worms. The others are just a few minutes behind."

Fost looked uneasily over his shoulder. This group of worms seemed to number more than a half dozen,

though with the worms twining together and swaying in
the uncertain light it was hard to tell. None was as large
as the patriarch Fost had slain, so perhaps he and
Moriana had a chance. But if the other worms came
upon them from behind while they were engaged, their
quest for eternal life would end here, fruitlessly.

The worms had recovered from the shock of meeting
light and advanced with their strange bulging-squeezing
movement. Their cilia glided like skates along the ice.
Moriana moved to meet them, scimitar in hand. Fost
followed.

"Hold," Erimenes said. "Let me out first. How can I
truly enjoy the shedding of blood—even rank, yellow
blood—all cooped up in this wretched flower pot? Release me."

Fost did. Time sped away, inevitable death hunched
nearer with each second and fear and battle lust filled
Fost with manic energy that could find release only in
combat. Yet he paused to draw Erimenes's jug from his
knapsack, unstop the vessel and stuff it back into the
bag as the blue vapor swirled forth.

Erimenes materialized at Fost's elbow as the courier
came to stand beside Moriana. Materialize was the
word, too, Fost thought. When he'd first seen the philosopher's shade out on the lonely steppe-road south of
Samadum, Erimenes was only a pallid wraith, virtually
invisible at times. Now he seemed more substantial,
almost solid. Had he not known better, Fost would
have believed the man beside him as corporeal as he or
Moriana, albeit blue.

"Why'd you let him out? I dislike having him leering
over my shoulder as I fight. It makes me feel unclean."
Moriana scowled past Fost at the spirit.

Fost shrugged. The worms came at them, and there
was no time for words.

One lunged for Moriana's throat. Her long knife caught it beneath the clacking jaws, the Sky City blade chopped down and the ugly head split open. Fost caught a glimpse of blue-shot yellow ganglia exposed by the wound. A worm attacked him then, and he had to concentrate on staying alive.

Side by side they fought, exiled princess and slumbred courier. Each swing of their swords sent droplets of gore spattering over the walls, the worms, their own fronts and faces. Fost's wounds, hastily bandaged, began to bleed anew. Both he and Moriana bore fresh raw marks where the worms' jaws had found them by the time the last monster was struck down.

But struck down they all were. Fost leaned against a wall, sword hanging limply, feeling sick and exhausted to the depths of his soul. He glanced at Moriana. Her lovely face was haggard and drawn beneath a viscous film of worm blood.

Erimenes crowed like a rutting cock at the sight of so much blood. Fost regarded him from sunken eyes. The inhuman gloating on the philosopher's ascetic face nauseated him as thoroughly as the reeking corpses of the worms.

From behind came a scrabbling noise, echoing starkly in the ice tunnel. The pair spun to see the first pursuing worm's head poke around the bend, shrink away from the light and then come on purposefully. Fost tapped Moriana's arm.

"Away," he said, hoarse with the reaction of bloodletting. "With any luck they'll stay awhile devouring their luckless comrades."

The hisses of the worms cut across the slapping of their bootsoles on ice. Then came the now-familiar tearing sound, and Fost turned his head back briefly to see the worms feeding with cannibalistic fervor. As he watched, two heads reared up and thrust at one another.

The beasts were fighting over the choicer remains of their kindred.

"That ought to hold them for a while," Fost said before a curve took them out of sight.

"A pity it won't delay them long enough," Erimenes sighed.

"Long enough for what?" demanded Moriana. Without breaking stride, she had pulled a rag from her knapsack and was vigorously scouring the filth from her face.

"I sense that battle has brought your sexual appetites to unparalleled keenness. What a pity you haven't time to shed your clothes and sate the hunger within your loins. What a striving that would be!"

Moriana snarled something at the spirit, who floated effortlessly alongside them. But her green eyes brushed Fost's grey ones, and she knew that for both of them the sage's words hit uncomfortably close to the truth.

They flew inward through the glacier. Erimenes glowed with a light to rival that of the torches, and the gold sparks that danced within him blazed like newborn suns. Moriana had passed Fost her pine splinter at the onset of the fight, and yellow flames streaked out behind him like a banner.

Abruptly the torch flared high. At the same instant Fost felt a breath of coolness wash over his face, not cool with the chill of the glacier's bowels but fresh and crisp, invigorating.

The tunnel bent and brought them face to face with beauty. It was a beauty so tangible that they stopped and blinked with wonder. Fost and Moriana gripped each other but didn't share a look. They couldn't take their eyes from the spectacle before them. Their lips worked, but it was Erimenes who gave name to the vision.

"Athalau," he said.

CHAPTER
EIGHT

Prince Rann's mount shrilled raucous response to the scouting bird in the sky ahead. His gaze scarcely less keen than the eagle's, Rann strained to see through the dying polar night. There, there it was. At the very foot of the ice sheet was the black smudge of a dead campfire.

The fugitives had made no attempt to cover their tracks after leaving the shelter of the mountains. Conceivably they thought no one pursued them any longer. Rann laughed at the thought.

To all intents and purposes the fugitives had simply marched up to the foot of the glacier and disappeared. Their tracks led to the looming ice cliff, blending into a muddle as though the two had spent hours pacing before the glacier. No tracks led away.

Rann circled his bird into a landing. Around him threescore bird-riders brought their mounts to frozen earth. The promised reinforcements had arrived promptly. The treacherous air currents had dashed two of the newcomers to bloody jam against the peaks and a sudden onslaught of thulyakhashawin had accounted for three more Sky Guardsmen. Rann suspected he'd feel their loss keenly during these next few hours.

A party of scouts clustered at the foot of the sheer, shiny cliff, weapons ready. They peered at the fire's remains, at the rocks the pair had sat upon, at the snow trampled by their feet, at the hundred-foot face of the glacier. Their worried looks told Rann they were as baffled as he.

He seated himself on a rock while more Guardsmen came to search. His tawny eyes stared out blankly across the Waste. The sun fell toward the waiting arms

189

of the Ramparts to the West, spilling its blood on the ice. Rann smiled a little within. Bloodstained beauty he could appreciate.

"Milord." A lieutenant crunched through snow to bend the knee before him. Bandy-legged Captain Tays had fallen at the fight in the mountains, his face crunched in the jaws of a huge black bear. Newly arrived Lieutenant Odon was now the prince's second-in-command.

"What have you to report?" Rann asked without looking at the man.

"Nothing, lord." The pale eyes fixed him like spears. "Nothing I could make sense of. Just that fissure."

"What about it?" Rann rose.

"I'll show you, lord." Odon led him to the glacier. Rann felt the chill emanating from it and felt thankful for the fur-trimmed cloaks the reinforcements had brought from the Sky City. He examined the crack indicated by the officer.

A rock was trapped at the base of the fissure. It didn't seem to have been overrun by the glacier's stately advance. The ice was splintered to either side of the rock as though the crack had opened briefly and slammed shut on it.

"Interesting." Rann nodded, fingering his chin. "Somehow the glacier opened to them, and they passed within, accidentally kicking this rock into the opening. I've wondered how Moriana hoped to reach the ice-locked city. Obviously she has some sorcery we know nothing of that enabled her to open this way."

Gloved fists beat his thighs. "Synalon has grown too complacent. She underestimates her sibling. Moriana has gained much power."

"Have we no spells to follow them, lord?"

"None." He spat the word out as if it tasted bitter. "We must dig our way inside, Lieutenant. Burrow after them like moles." He shook his head. "It will take too long. *Too long.*"

"But, lord," the officer protested, "all we have to dig with are our weapons. Working the ice will blunt their edges."

Rann turned toward him. In his eyes dwelled a chill deeper than the ice. "Then you will dig until they break. Then you will burrow with your fingernails until they break too, and then with your fingers till they wear to bloody nubs. After that you can chew the ice with your teeth. But dig you will, until we reach Athalau. Do I make myself clear?"

"Y-yes, lord."

Rann nodded curtly and turned away as the troopers attacked the ice with sword and spear. Steel bit with brittle sound, sending splinters and flakes flying like bits of diamond.

"Who pecks at me?" a voice drawled.

The digging stopped. The men backed from the glacier, weapons dropping from fear-numbed hands. Startled, Rann looked at the glacier. Unquestionably the words had issued from the very ice. He'd heard tales of inanimate things, rocks and ice, given life in the confrontation between the Earth-Spirit and the demon. Always he had attributed the stories to too-strong ale rather than the War of Powers. He had been wrong. He had little trouble adjusting to the fact; he wasn't a man to let preconceptions hold sway over solid evidence.

"You, glacier," he said. "You guard the city of Athalau?"

"I am Guardian."

"I beg your leave to enter with my men."

The waiting seconds pulled Rann's nerves ever tauter. He envisioned Moriana and her leman nearing their goal. If they gained it, it would bring disaster upon Synalon's plans—and what befell her befell him. He wanted to scream at the glacier to hurry. He knew it would do no good.

"A millennium passes without human feet ever venturing this way," the glacier said at length. "Now in a single blink of the sun's eye I encounter many. Why?"

"I seek my cousin. Her tracks lead here and stop. Did you admit her and her companion?"

"I admitted her with companions." The booming voice emphasized the plural. "She had a dark-haired man with the air of Northern heat and haste about him and the shade of one who dwelled here within the city long ago. I felt it unkind to deny entry to an Athalar, and the lady was of that kindred, also." It paused endlessly. "You say you are her cousin. The blood of Athalau blesses your veins too, does it not?"

"Why, yes, yes indeed. I seek to aid her in her quest."

"I wondered why your party was so large." The glacier mused another thirteen minutes. "Hmmm. Such a force could slay many ice-worms."

"What?"

"Ice-worms. The vermin infest me. They itch most abominably. I allowed your cousin and her friends inside on condition they slay as many of the pests as possible. But there were only two who could fight, the third being incorporeal, and the worms are strong and wily beasts. I doubt they can account for many."

"We will account for scores of ice-worms, my men and I!"

"And you will wreak no harm in sacred Athalau?"

Rann laughed. "I will do nothing Moriana herself would not."

"Very well," the glacier said. Again it opened with an earthshattering noise. Rann called Maguerr to him. Loath though he was to rely on the pimpled journeyman, he needed to maintain a link with the outside world. Quickly he instructed the youth to stay behind with five men to tend the war birds and, every hour, look in on the prince by means of the seeing stone. At this short range the fledgling mage could communicate via the geode without Rann requiring one of his own. That done, the prince drew blade and led his men into the yawning crack.

The bird-riders looked uneasily at the sides of the crevice. It was as if immense jaws swallowed them, jaws that could snap shut at any instant. As if to emphasize the fact, the walls shook, dropping jagged ice fragments from above on the hurrying file of men.

"Ahead of you lies an ice-worm tunnel," came the glacier's voice from all around the Sky City men. "That way went your friends. You must reach it soon. I cannot hold the passageway open much longer."

Rann shouted his troops into a run. The trembling of the walls was becoming more pronounced, and the last of the bird-riders had only just entered the glacier. He set the pace and quickly found he must take short, mincing steps to avoid going down on his back due to the slippery surface. Shouts and curses from behind told him others were making the same discovery.

The walls slid inward. Men screamed. But the looming faces of the crevice did not slam together. Sweating, Rann gained the ice-worm tunnel and dashed into it. Behind him came the Guardsmen in a mad scramble.

A grating sound crunched from the walls. Ice shook beneath Rann's feet. The crack closed with such force that the bird-riders were thrown to the tunnel floor. Shrieks rose, suddenly wild, to be cut off by the doomsday slam of the walls coming together.

Rann hauled himself up. Sweat froze on his face. "Count off!" he bawled. At his side, Lieutenant Odon echoed his cry.

Struggling to their feet, the men obeyed. Rann listened stonily in the darkness that had descended as the numbers rolled back in the now-sealed mouth of the tunnel. The counting went to twenty-nine.

And stopped.

Rann ground his teeth together. He had lost half of his men at a single stroke.

"Glacier," he called, "may we light torches?"

At the reluctant affirmative, lights flared in the passageway. Rann glanced at the bluish ice that had shut off the entrance of the worm path. A red ooze trickled to the floor of the tunnel.

"Move out," he grated.

Grumbles rose at his back. "He spends our lives like sipans!" a trooper muttered.

Rann turned back, his grin a death's-head. "Aye, and what of it? What will your lives—and mine—be worth if Moriana escapes with the amulet?" The looks on the bird-riders' faces told him he'd made his point. They knew nothing of what the amulet did, for that wasn't knowledge to be entrusted to a common soldier. But they knew their queen desired it, and they knew how Synalon served those whose failure thwarted her desires. Shaken and pale, they readied their weapons and followed their leader.

The eunuch-prince strode as rapidly as he dared. He felt the men's gazes burning into his back. Their hatred for him crackled in the air like lightning about to strike. It didn't worry him. Men might claim to love a commander who treated them well and never spent their lives when he could avoid it but they never truly respected him. Rann didn't care for their love but he commanded their fear. Nor did their welfare concern him; he was troubled by the loss of over thirty men but only because he feared he might need their numbers soon. The survivors loathed him for his callousness, but they followed him closely. They had marched into the depths of a cold, living hell. Only a resolute, utterly ruthless man like Rann stood any chance of leading them out again.

Odon walked a pace behind his leader. Rann felt him hovering and looked back with eyebrow raised.

"The ice-worms, lord," Odon said. His voice shook, and his skin shone faintly green in the light of the torches. Apparently the thought of a score and a half of his comrades being squashed to paste bothered him.

"What about them?"

"Should we be looking for them, lord? We promised Guardian, after all."

Rann eyed him coldly. He wondered how this pup had ever come by a commission in the Sky Guard. He was too soft for the *corps d'élite*.

"We hunt Moriana, Fost Longstrider and the spirit. Nothing else. If we encounter ice-worms, then we'll deal with them. We'll waste no time seeking them out."

Odon seemed ready to protest tricking Guardian. The look on Rann's scarred face silenced him. He swallowed his objections, finally saying, "How will we follow the fugitives, lord?"

Rann pointed ahead. "We'll find some sign up there, I believe."

Odon's gaze followed the finger. Yellow blood and fragments of rubbery flesh were all that remained of some unidentifiable creature. The stench made even Rann's head swim. Something had died violently and been devoured here at the junction of two ice-worm tunnels. Rann went into the cross-passage, stooped and smiled with satisfaction.

"Indeed, indeed," he said to himself. He rose to follow a trail of red drops into the heart of the living glacier.

"I've never seen anything like it," Moriana said.

"Of course you haven't," Erimenes said. "For this is

Athalau, and there is none to compare with her." His voice rang with genuine pride.

Looking at the City in the Glacier, Fost couldn't feel that that pride was misplaced. Athalau was indeed incomparable. Neither Tolviroth Acerte nor the Sky City possessed anything near the simple elegance of Athalau, and deep inside Fost felt sure that even High Medurim in her prime was a slum compared to this.

There were none of the gauds and bangles his imagination had come to expect: no streets paved with gold, no jewel-encrusted façades on the buildings. But each and every structure in the great city was a work of art, each possessing its own essence and its own charm, yet all blended into a harmonious whole. Towers rose dizzyingly higher than any Fost had ever seen, and thin spires beside them buttressed them with a spiderweb of finely wrought stone or metal. Colonnades marched solemnly along the avenues between domes whose very curves were poetry. Off in the middle distance a minaret loomed high above the rest, and here at least was evidence of the city's fabulous wealth, for it was carved from a single ruby. The city glowed with a light of its own, shifting, sourceless, containing all the colors of the rainbow and implying a myriad more.

Not all was perfection, as the courier and the princess saw when the first rush of awe subsided. The ice of the glacier formed a high dome above the city, as though Athalau lay in a gigantic stomach. At one time even the regal Ruby Tower had been well clear of the icy roof. But over the years icicles like stalactites had flowed down from the vault of the glacier and stalagmites of frozen water grew to meet them. Some of the structures in sight were cased in rippling sheaths of ice. Elsewhere great chunks of ice had fallen, crushing masonry.

Moriana was the first to shake free of the spell. "We must hurry," she said. "I feel danger all around."

"Some people simply aren't cut out to be travelers," Erimenes said severely. "You merely suffer a foreigner's distaste for the unfamiliar."

Fost looked around warily. The tunnel had given way to a ledge of ice that sloped gently until it reached the outermost buildings of Athalau. A hundred yards away on their left lay a fallen stalactite of ice a hundred feet long and twenty feet thick at the large end. It had broken into neat segments as though split by a gargantuan woodcutter's axe.

"Having eighty tons of ice land on my head would be unfamiliar, spirit, and I confess I'd find the experience shattering."

Erimenes lifted his nose. He looked more and more like a real, living being. "That shaft fell centuries ago," he said disdainfully.

"Perhaps another's overdue," said Fost.

"Hist." Moriana raised her hand, her face suddenly taut and distant. "I hear something."

Fost closed his eyes and concentrated, screening out the sounds of their breathing. He heard it too, a rumbling of different timbre than the internal groanings of the glacier, an intermittent clicking sound and, rising and falling at their hair's-breadth of perception, the babble of voices.

"I hear them too." Moriana frowned, her hand falling to rest on the hilt of her sword.

"Rann?" asked Fost.

"Who else?"

"But how did he get in?"

Erimenes stood with one hand cupped theatrically to his ear. "It is Rann in truth, with more than a score of men," he said. "As to how he gained entrance, I fear Guardian is less, uh, perceptive than one might wish."

"In other words Rann talked his way in the same as we did." Fost scowled. "A fine set of circumstances."

"Come," Moriana said. "Let's get down to the city. We should be able to reach the Amulet of Living Flame before they arrive."

Fost bit his lip at the name. That final question still lay between him and Moriana: Whose should the amulet be? She still seemed willing to defer finding an answer. So would he—for now.

"How to proceed?" he asked.

"We haven't much choice, unless you can climb these icy inclines." Erimenes gestured. The slope ahead of them was hollowed out into a sort of run that reached down to the city. Steep walls curved up to either side.

"What made it that way?" asked Moriana. "It looks worn down. Could worms have done it sliding down into Athalau from the tunnel?"

"Of course not!" Erimenes's face showed outrage. "Even such as they realize what a desecration that would be. They remain in their burrows, devouring one another."

Fost looked dubious. But Erimenes was right, at least in that they had little choice of how to go. They started gingerly down the slope. Fost took three steps and then lost his balance, his legs flying out from under him. His tailbone hit with an impact that brought tears to his eyes. Immediately he was whizzing down the hill toward Athalau.

He heard Moriana's alarmed shout behind him turn instantly to a laugh of pure glee. She zipped past him, likewise seated with her knees drawn to her chin, stroking at the ice to go even faster.

"Unfair!" shouted Fost. Laughing, he pushed himself in pursuit. As they reached bottom, he caught up with her, seized her around the waist and sent them both sprawling in a laughing tangle on the street.

"My rump is glowing hot!" Moriana cried, rumpling Fost's black hair.

He kissed her soundly. "I'll agree to that," he said, reaching and squeezing. "Perhaps some fresh air will cool it off." He tugged at her breeches.

"Ahem." Erimenes's lordly throat-clearing drew their attention. "Might I suggest you postpone your recreation to a more suitable time and place? Prince Rann approaches."

Fost and Moriana grinned at each other, disentangled themselves and stood. They knew that their momentary distraction had arisen from the strain they were under. They couldn't afford another such lapse. Nonetheless they were still grinning when Fost took Moriana's hand and they set off up the street.

The boulevards of Athalau were paved with some mysterious smooth substance, hard like stone but which flowed continuously, showing no telltale seams between blocks. To Fost's mind this was nearly as wondrous as streets of gold would have been.

The smile faded from his face. Erimenes had urged them to forget their loveplay and get on with the business at hand— Erimenes! The lecherous, long-dead virgin who would propose they fornicate in the middle of a hornbull stampede. Fost shook his head. There was something very wrong here.

They entered a new block and halted. Sinuous shapes glided out of buildings into the street. A familiar hissing filled the air.

"So they won't desecrate holy Athalau," Fost said bitterly, glaring at Erimenes. "What are those— heretics?"

Erimenes's eyes bulged at the worms. A half a hundred had poured from the lovely ruins like maggots from a gilded skull. "I must—that is—this is certainly an unforeseen circumstance."

Deliberately Fost slid his sword from its sheath. "I've a mind to lob your jug to them, Erimenes. A worm's gizzard is a fitting resting place for such as you."

Erimenes gibbered in terror. Moriana laid a hand on her lover's arm.

"Not yet. Erimenes, can you affect the ice-worms' minds?"

"They haven't minds enough!"

"But you can still work your invisibility trick on Rann's men?"

"Yes," Erimenes said. "But it's not merely a trick. It is mental manipulation of the most sophisticated . . ."

"Enough, Erimenes. Fost, can you delay the worms a few minutes?" Fost looked at her, nodded slowly. "Good. Hold them here. I'm going to have a talk with Rann."

"You're going to parley with that eunuch-bastard?" he grated angrily.

"Not exactly." She started away, then paused. "The satchel. You wouldn't . . ."

"If you mean, would I go on without you to find the amulet, I would not even if the worms let me." He flicked his eyes toward the approaching worms. Fifty yards still separated them from the humans. "As to whether I'll let you take the satchel, the answer is likewise no."

She looked hard at him, nodded and was off, running back the way they had come. He watched her, wondering whether she wasn't hoping to work some deal with her cousin. He shook his head. *I grow too distrustful. The thought's unworthy of me.* He faced the worms.

Moriana heard harsh voices echoing in the huge dome that enclosed the city. She came out at the foot of the street that led to the ice run. A group of men stood clustered around the tunnel mouth. The soft glow of the city looked strange reflected from their naked weapons. Their garb was black and purple, but even without that she would have known the slim, erect figure that stood to one side, surveying the city.

"Rann!" she called. The figure looked at her and went deathly still. "Half-man, coward, traitorous offal. Come and get me, if you have the courage!"

Even at this distance she could feel his rage. Her voice echoed, amplified by the vastness of the chamber. Somewhere vibrations broke loose a giant icicle and it came crashing down. Ignoring it, Rann broke into a run toward her, bellowing to his men to follow. Moriana stood a moment longer, waiting. Rann managed to keep his feet to the bottom of the run, though none of his men did. Moriana spun and fled like a deer.

Arrows whistled in pursuit. None came near. Making sure she was in sight of the Guardsmen, she led them straight toward the block where Fost faced the ice-worms.

She rounded the corner. Fost looked back at the sound of her footsteps. A worm lay dead before him, his now useless torch buried in its brain. Another writhed in its death-throes nearby.

"Fost!" Moriana shouted. "This way!"

He turned, saw her and raced for her. Sensing victory, the ice-worms slid in pursuit, their hissing more chilling than the glacier's cold. By dint of furious leg-work Fost gained twenty yards on them by the time he reached the waiting princess.

"Erimenes, make us invisible. Use your mind trick, now!" Moriana cried.

"Certainly," the spirit said. "But I must insist . . ."

"And in the name of the Five Holy Ones Who Died for Athalau, be quiet!"

The baying voices of the Guardsmen came nearer. Fost and Moriana hugged each other, not daring to breathe. Would Erimenes's spell work? Or would he betray them to a terrible death?

A youth, long-legged for a bird-rider and wearing an officer's silver gorget, pelted around the corner an arm's length from the fugitives. At the sight of the worms he halted. Then the rest swept onto the street, and their momentum bore him and them straight into the tangle of worms.

Men cried out in pain and fear. Ice-worms blew their foul breath. The Guardsmen fought savagely, but the ice-worms outnumbered them. Man-blood and worm-blood ran in rivers, blending into a ghastly puree that sizzled and steamed in the cold.

Unseen and all but forgotten, Fost and Moriana slipped from the doorway. They had no cause to feel compassion for the bird-riders, but still the scene appalled them. The worms were tearing the soldiers apart. Black jaws severed arms at a bite, legs thrashed air as toothed maws shredded half-swallowed men. The battle could have but one outcome.

Only Erimenes's no longer spectral face showed triumph as they made their way around the corner and away.

CHAPTER
NINE

Hand in hand Fost and Moriana walked through glory. A glory tarnished by time, to a certain extent, with scars showing where ice-worms had laired in buildings or ice had plummeted from above, but glory nonetheless.

Erimenes floated beside them. He was a small, slender man with a long head, receding hair and a blade of a nose above thin lips. Fost wondered if he put his hand out whether or not it would pass through the spirit or meet the resistance of solid flesh. Beyond the specks of gold light that swirled through him, the only evidence of Erimenes's nature was his feet— or the lack of them. His skinny legs ended in a swirl of dense blue fog from which an indigo umbilicus extended to the pot, which rode at Fost's hip.

"Now you must do the service you promised us, Erimenes," said Fost. "Only you know the resting place of the Amulet of Living Flame." Moriana's hand squeezed convulsively in his at the mention of the name. He felt a hot flush creep up his neck.

Erimenes nodded, smiling. "That I do. It hangs in the nave of the Palace of Esoteric Wisdom, foremost structure in all of Athalau."

They hurried along broad thoroughfares toward the center of the swallowed city. The shifting light suffused them with a sense of well-being but it couldn't overcome their urgency to reach the end of their quest.

"How much farther is it?" Moriana asked.

"The world unravels itself around you, and you have thought for nothing save yourselves." Erimenes shook his head. "Great were the Athalar but they are done, dust. I alone remain to appreciate the splendor of what once was."

Fost growled warningly.

"Very well," the philosopher said. "Another turning of the way and you shall behold the Palace with your own eyes."

Unconsciously the pair quickened their pace. The pavement underfoot was solid enough but seemed to lend spring to their steps. Hearts hammering, they turned the final corner.

A broad square stretched before them. In its center rested a fountain, its tongue of waters long stilled, an abstract of silent tiers. At the far end of the plaza the tower of ruby flowed upward, the fineness of its lines giving it the illusion of movement and flight.

"The Palace of Esoteric Wisdom," Fost breathed in awe.

To his astonishment, Erimenes shook his head. "You are deceived. Poor are you in wisdom. This way, to your left. I shall guide you, never fear." Chuckling to himself, the spirit led the way.

Puzzled, the two followed. The carved gem tower was the most impressive work of architecture either had ever seen. How could it be other than the "foremost structure in Athalau"?

Erimenes signed them to a halt. "Here, children. Here lies the Palace. Within its sacred precincts awaits eternal life. And more, aye, ever so much more." He chortled as if enjoying some private jest.

Fost stared at the building. He blinkly slowly. The structure stayed the same.

"How can this be?" he demanded. Far from the soaring wonder he had anticipated, the Palace of Esoteric Wisdom was a simple basilica of snowy marble, fronted with a portico upheld by columns as devoid of decoration as the rest of the edifice. Its doorway was a single pointed arch, as were the windows of the clerestory.

Silver light danced in the windows. "It's a handsome building, without elaborations or fripperies as you'd find in decadent Medurim. But to call this the foremost?" He shook his head in disgust.

Erimenes looked severe. "I wonder why you seek everlasting life so assiduously. You lack the discrimination truly to enjoy it. Hear wisdom, child, though scant is my hope that you'll heed it: That which is of the most worth is not necessarily the gaudiest to behold."

Fost sneered, but Moriana touched his arm and said, "He may be right. I myself enjoy ornateness, but something in the cleanness of this place's lines beguiles the eye."

"If you find it so pleasing," a voice said from behind them, "by all means fill your eyes with it, for it is the last sight they shall behold."

"Rann!" The name broke from Moriana in a choked cry.

"The same. My gratitude, cousin, for leading me to the Amulet of Living Flame."

Fost and Moriana drew their blades. The bird-riders spread out into a semicircle to hem them against the edifice, five to either side of the prince.

"How did you escape the worms, half-man?" Moriana asked.

"I left half the men to deal with the worms." Rann's lips tensed into a grin. "My men had informed me of the invisibility trick you used to elude them in the ravines. When you lured us into the worms and slipped away, I guessed what you were doing. I managed to extricate these men and come after you. I had a feeling our mutual goal would be somewhere in the very heart of Athalau. So we hid and waited for you."

"You're a coward as well as a gelding," Fost spat. "To desert your own men!"

"They gave their lives for the Sky City and its queen. It was an honor I gave them." The soldiers approached slowly, tightening the net. Rann had pulled out none too soon by the looks of them. Hardly a man didn't bear the marks of the black-gleaming chitin jaws. But their faces were hard with determination, and madness glinted behind their eyes.

They charged. Fost met an upward thrust with a stop-thrust to the forearm. The bird-rider dropped his blade, cursing. Even as he staggered back, Fost's blade swept around him and streaked to the heart of a second attacker.

Moriana stood exchanging deft wrist cuts with a brown-haired trooper whose left arm was missing below the elbow. A ragged, bloodstained bandage wrapped the stump. Moriana flicked her sword at his temple. His blade winked up to parry. Moriana's arm pivoted and brought her sword down to *chunk!* into the man's un-armored side. With a blood-frothing moan he sank to his knees. Moriana sprang past him to engage another.

Fost found himself facing Rann. The prince showed his teeth in a smile.

"You are brave and strong," Rann grunted, easily turning back Fost's powerful attacks. "We could amuse each other many a long hour, you and I. I am sorry that you must quickly . . . *die!*"

Like a serpent the scimitar flashed past Fost's guard, striking for his heart. He swung his right side forward and groaned as the point took him in the shoulder. He leaped away. Crimson gleamed on the blade as it slid out. Rann lunged again. The thrust lacked strength; Fost's mail stopped it, though it bruised his breastbone. He hacked with the strength of pain-born fury. Rann's sword warded off the blow, but it laid open the prince's cheek and sent him reeling back.

A sword whistled by Moriana's ear, so near it snipped a lock of golden hair. She bled from cuts in her thigh and arm. She danced back as her enemy drove at her, howling with fury.

He stopped, eyes black circles of amazement in his skull-white face. Moriana stared back, mind staggered by the hammerblow of recognition. "Odon!" she gasped. "My friend in my youth, what are you doing here?"

"Lady," he said, his mouth working like a fish's. "Oh, lady, I am sorry. . . ." His hand came up, sword aimed as duty overcame sentiment. She read his intent. Her sword ripped out his throat like the claw of a beast. He died with his eyes fixed on her. Tears fogged her own as two more men engaged her.

By unspoken agreement the bird-riders let their leader have the big Northland courier to himself. Fost hadn't fared so well the last time he'd crossed swords with Rann and he wasn't eager to face the prince again. Though healed by Jennas's poultices, the wound in his thigh began to throb as if recalling the last encounter.

Fost had the advantage of strength and reach over the small Sky City noble and he wore the mail vest the bear-folk had given him, while Rann had no protection beyond his heavy cloak. On his side the prince had speed, lesser size and—much as Fost hated to admit it—greater skill. They came together again, blades splashing the soft glow of the city in streaks across their sweating faces, singing the mating song of steel.

Back and back the prince forced Fost. Occasionally a massive blow by Fost made the eunuch give way instead, but the great overpowering sweep left Fost's body exposed. After a lightning riposte laid open his hauberk and the belly beneath, Fost let well enough alone and concentrated on fighting a delaying action.

He tried to break for the door of the Palace. A grinning trio of Sky Guardsmen blocked him. His flowing wounds had sapped him of strength. He lacked the power for the berserk charge that would have bowled them over and let him through.

"Kill!" a voice cried. Fost's eyes snapped to his side. Forgotten, Erimenes stood by, clapping spectral hands in glee. "Oh, the blood. Never has Athalau known such a spectacle!"

"Erimenes, make us invisible," Fost cried. Taking advantage of the distraction, Rann lunged—and pulled up short, a puzzled look on his face.

Then comprehension glowed in his eyes. His sword licked out. Fost gasped as it sliced at his left biceps.

"Your blood," the prince said, "falls to the pavement and reveals your presence. A moment now and we'll let the rest out."

Undaunted by his foe's invisibility, he came in, his sword a sighing whirlwind of death. Beyond him Fost saw Moriana likewise being driven to the wall by a jeering half-ring of foes. Though he could see her, they could not. Like Rann they traced her by the drops of blood she shed.

Five Sky City men were out of the fight, but the odds remained three to one against Fost and Moriana. Weakened as they were, they couldn't hold out much longer.

"Erimenes," Fost shouted in desperation. "Aid us! Have you no other powers that can help?"

Standing beside him, not changing his gleeful expression when an occasional sword cut slashed through his torso, Erimenes nodded. "Many are my powers," he said. "Watch."

At the very apex of the ice dome, half a thousand feet overhead, the glacier was latticed with deep cracks. The shifting and endless motion of the glacier had weakened the ice over the years. Now a great block hung barely suspended, ready to break away at any instant.

The pull of mental power from below was slight. But it sufficed.

A rumbling brought Fost's eyes up. "Back!" he screamed to Moriana. "Against the wall!" He drove at Rann with all his strength. Taken by surprise, Rann was caught high in the left breast. He stumbled back, sword slipping from his hands. His gaze followed Fost's.

He bellowed in rage and pain as thirty tons of ice engulfed him and his men.

For a moment Fost could do no more than stand with his forehead resting in his palm. Then Moriana was beside him, clutching him, kissing him.

"We won," she said, eyes disbelieving.

"With Erimenes's help. Did you bring the ice down, spirit?"

"Oh yes, yes, I did indeed. Of course it was almost ready to fall, else I should not have been able to budge it. But yes, my powers brought the ice block crashing down upon our foes." A sudden thought brightened his countenance. "Say, that means I killed them, didn't I? I, a spirit, shed the blood of living mortals. Oh, this is a great day!"

Fost gnawed his lip. Myriad red streams trickled out from under the ice, scarlet threads weaving a tapestry on the pavement. He saw little to gloat over in the spirit's loss of innocence.

"My thanks, spirit, for what they're worth."

He and Moriana supported each other up the steps into the Palace. It was a scramble at first. The falling block had shorn off the front of the portico and obstructed the foot of the steps, so the travelers had to climb up the side to gain the entrance. Still unimpressed by the Palace, Fost had to admit the Athalar had built well. Except where the ice had hit, the portico was undamaged. The pillars weren't even cracked. Painfully the two mounted the steps and pushed at the single copper door.

It swung open easily. They stepped inside. At first their eyes were dazzled by the quicksilver coruscations that met them. Then vision cleared.

"The amulet," Fost said, scarcely able to move his lips.

The nave of the Palace was fifty yards long, yet the altar seemed only the length of an arm away. A pendant hung from a black marble stand by a silver chain, a great gem set in a silver sunburst. The silver glow pulsed from the white jewel.

White? Fost thought. *Was it not black as midnight a heartbeat ago?* Almost invisible in the shine of the radiant gem, a second amulet hung beside it, a poor thing hardly more than a polished grey stone knotted to a leather thong. Fost was amazed to see such dross so near such magnificence.

Moriana started forward as if in a trance, fingers stretching toward the brilliant, half-black, half-white gem. Fost caught her arm with iron fingers. She turned on him, eyes hot and angry.

"Let me go!" she spat. "I must have the amulet. My people groan beneath my sister's heel."

"No!" Fost dragged her face to his. "I have suffered, bled and almost died on your behalf. How would you have fared if I'd left you to the Vicar of Istu?"

Rage was shaken from her by a tremor of revulsion. The green balefire died from her eyes. She slumped in the big man's grip. "Ill," she admitted, dropping her gaze. "Even now I'd be trapped in the mind of the sleeping Demon, prey to his every horrid fantasy, and damnation would seem the purest of blessings."

He let her go. He felt ashamed. *But life, life everlasting! I cannot let that go!*

"I'll take the amulet," he said quietly. "It's mine. It is only right, don't you see?" The woman nodded convulsively. Tears shone on her cheeks. "There, I'm sorry. I . . . I'll help you fight your sister. How's that? I'll aid you in overthrowing Synalon. Everything will work out, don't you see? But, but I must have the amulet." He finished with his hands cupping the air in front of him, spreading them in a lame gesture.

"I understand," she whispered. "I . . . I'll say no more about it."

He nodded briskly. A little spirit seeped back into him. It's difficult for gloom to keep a grasp on a man with immortality within his reach.

He walked to the altar. Erimenes and Moriana followed like shadows in that shadowless place. Not even the pillars flanking the nave cast shadows into the walkways beyond. The floor, blocks of black marble interspersed with white, thumped like a drum under their boots.

Visions filled his head as he neared the mostly-white jewel. A lifetime—many lifetimes—to spend or squander as he would. Drinking, wenching, fighting his way through rollicking centuries. And more than that. He would make a fortune, a dozen fortunes, return to Medurim as equal to the wealthy to whom he'd once been less than filth. He would devote the span of a dozen natural lives to gleaning the untold wealth from the libraries of the ancient city, wealth he but glimpsed before. All knowledge lay open to his questing hand. He could be the world's wisest man, as well as its doughtiest warrior.

So caught up was he in his imaginings that he didn't notice how his steps slowed until they stopped completely.

"What's this?" he asked aloud. His jaw moved slowly, as though dipped in glue. He tried to raise his foot. It felt rooted to the marble. "Moriana, what treachery is this?" The words came as slowly as Guardian's speech.

"None of mine, I swear it," the princess said, her voice a slow roll of molasses.

Fost's head weighed tons, but he forced it round to bear on Erimenes. A whirlwind of suns shone from his blue body.

"Spirit," Fost said thickly. "This is your doing."

"Naturally." Erimenes beamed.

Fost's lips formed the word *why?*

"How can you ask?" The aquiline face twisted with fury. "You stupid, selfish, senseless clod! I would have what you so blithely take for granted, what you so obdurately fail to appreciate. I would have life—true life! Yes, you understand, I read it in your eyes!

"The amulet gives the blessing of life. It will return me to my body. No more being dependent upon the whim of other, lesser beings for my sensation. I will take life in my own two hands and wring it until its sweet juices pour down my throat." He raised his hands before him, shaking with passion. "I will still live forever, with the amulet's aid. But I shall have a body that sees and smells and feels—aye, and lusts." He laughed a sad laugh. "Oh, dear Fost, dear Moriana, how could you be so foolish to believe I'd let you have the Amulet of Living Flame?"

"What happens to us?" Moriana asked. It was a struggle even to utter the words. "I feel the cold entering my bones. Soon we will freeze."

"No, you won't. You're young and strong, resilient. I shall take the amulet and restore my body. Then I'll tie you, though not so well that you can't in time escape, and leave you to your own devices. There's a good deal of treasure about, of a more mundane variety. Content yourselves with that." He turned toward the altar, busily rubbing his hands together. "Now, Fost, my good man, reach out and bring the amulet to my jar."

The man's arm did not lift of its own accord. It stretched toward the amulets hanging from the altar. His eyes followed its progress. Then his gaze slid past it to the blazing gem.

Amulet of Living Flame, he thought. *It's mine. Mine.* MINE!

His hand stopped. "What's this?" Erimenes demanded. "Are you trying to resist me? Come, come, my man. It can't be done. I am at the center of my power. Give in and save yourself the effort."

Fost frowned. The jewel burned like a sun within his brain. The black eclipsed the white. He ground his jaws together. He recalled the way Erimenes had controlled his limbs near the city of the Ethereals and the softly insidious ways the Ethereals trapped his mind. He recalled the helpless horror the way the tentacled thing, hideous and lovely, had wrapped him in the chains of temptation. And he remembered what had saved him then, starting with a spark within, growing, expanding, eating at his limbs, his rage like a spreading conflagration. . . .

Anger!

It drove the creeping cold from his limbs, the lethargy that settled on his brain. *Come, rage, consume me and give me strength!* he thought. His eyes were fixed on the jewel. The fury built, and did the white push away the black?

He saw Erimenes's face twisted in anguish. He saw Moriana's lovely features slack with awe. But before all he saw the jewel, its silver fire feeding his rage, the blackness, yes, the blackness giving way like the shadow of the moon after an eclipse.

His hands backed from the amulet. Erimenes's fingers flew to his temples and clung like spiders. Slowly

Fost fought his hand down toward his waist, the satchel, the jug. *Eternal life. He tries to cheat you. Remember!*

His fingers touched the basalt plug. Erimenes shrieked like one damned. The jewel blazed blinding white within Fost's brain. With a muscle-cracking heave he thrust the plug into the mouth of the spirit jar.

"*Noooooooooo!*" the spirit screamed as he faded from sight. "Fost! Don't do this to me! I must touch the amulet, I must! I am so weak, so weak!" His voice died to a sobbing lament.

Air gusted from Fost's lungs. He seemed to deflate, falling to his knees on the cold stone. Still the sun-stone burned in his mind. *Life, life, life everlasting!* Did he say the words or merely think them?

It took all his strength, but he made it to his feet. His hand stretched out, and this time it was of his own desire.

Agony exploded in his heart.

His hand jerked closed spasmodically. His fingers brushed past the radiant jewel to clamp around the rude stone pendant. He turned, feeling his legs dissolve beneath him.

Moriana stood, and Fost saw his own heart's blood dripping from the knife in her hand.

"Fost, I love you—but I must have the amulet. Tell me you understand. Oh please, my darling, *tell me you understand.*" Her words came from far away, an infinity away, across a chasm of endless dark.

The dark encompassed him, drew tight like a noose and narrowed his vision to a single point: Moriana's face, beautiful, grieving, lost.

Then Fost Longstrider died.

CHAPTER TEN

Fost sprawled in the gracelessness of death before the altar of the Palace of Esoteric Wisdom. The stone amulet rested like an offering in the center of his chest. His eyes gaped at the ceiling, framing the last of all questions.

Moriana fell weeping to her knees. She covered her face with her hands. The courier's blood had drenched them, and they turned her features to a crimson mask.

"Oh, Fost. Oh, my only love."

"Hypocritical bitch," came weakly from the jug.

"Be silent!" she shrieked, beating gory hands on the satchel.

"Why? Haven't I ample reason for complaint? I have lost my chance to live again. Oh, ashes, ashes!"

"I have lost my love." She sat back, wiping tears from her eyes. The first frenzy of remorse had calmed, leaving emptiness and aching.

"Love." Erimenes snorted. "A deadly way you have of showing it. More like a spider than a woman. What happens now? Do you eat the body?"

The princess rose. "I'll have no more of you, spirit." She went to the altar, picked up the glowing amulet and looped the chain around her neck. She held the gem in her palm. An electric tingle passed through her body. The jewel shone black like a dark sun. She sighed and let it drop between her breasts. Its touch chilled her.

She turned to kneel by Fost's body. Foolish hope brought fingertips to his throat, seeking any faint thread of pulse. There was none. She gently closed his eyelids and crossed his hands over his chest and the grey stone that rested there.

Tears spattered the lifeless face as she bent to kiss him. "Farewell, beloved," she said, her voice cracking like clay in the hot sun. "I promise you shall not have died in vain. When I have freed my City, and sent my sister shrieking to hell to join her eunuch lackey Rann, I will return and erect a shrine here to your memory."

"I'm sure that will bring him solace," Erimenes said acidly.

Moriana rose and turned her back. "I hope you will enjoy his company here until the sun itself receives Hell Call." Fighting to hold in her sobs, she began to walk away.

"Wait," Erimenes called. "Don't go! You can't leave me here!"

"Fost deserves better company than yours, faithless one," she said. "Still, here you will stay to guard over his body until my return. And ever after as well, accursed spirit."

"Don't be hasty." The philosopher's voice turned to honey. "I know something yet that could be of advantage to you. . . ."

Moriana paused, then fled, the tears streaming down her cheeks, the amulet beating like a second heart between her breasts. Erimenes called after her, voice rising in desperation. Only the echoing silence of Athalau answered him.

Silence settled in the chamber. Hours made soft transition from future to past. Then, dimly, sound encroached upon the stillness. It started as a rustling, grew to a dry crackling, became at last a rushing roar. A blue glow oozed between Fost's fingers. It seeped out to cover him, leaping ceilingward in a sudden wild dance.

Fost opened his eyes to flames. *Am I in hell?* he thought. Fire wrapped him in pain. A shuddering inhalation filled his lungs with flame. An incandescent point seared the flesh of his chest and ate into his palm. He snatched away the hand and sat up beating at the flames.

They were gone. He looked down at his chest. The mail had been burned away in a perfect circle. Yet the flesh beneath was not charred. An angry round red mark glowed there, but the skin was intact. To the side the rent left by the ice-worm's teeth exposed unmarked skin.

He blinked and shook his head to clear it. Gradually memories seeped into his skull. His eyes widened in astonishment.

"I . . . live," he mumbled. "I live!"

"A brilliant observation," a voice said at his elbow. "I didn't think you had it in you."

"Erimenes?"

"Who else? Certainly not that backstabbing slut of yours. She took the other amulet and left you for dead."

"Other amulet?" echoed Fost.

"The Destiny Stone, which hung next to the Amulet of Living Flame."

"Which hung beside . . ." his words trailed off. He stared stupidly at the satchel.

"Yes, fool. Your beloved princess stabbed you straight through the heart. You died, and in dying seized the amulet. Moriana took what you both assumed to be the Amulet of Living Flame."

Fost felt his back gingerly. There it was, the tear in the mail her dagger had made on its way to his heart. He felt a twinge of admiration for her. It took a strong hand and a sure one to drive a knife through linked rings of steel.

He stood. His knees felt like springs. He swayed, then steadied himself against the altar with one hand while the other brushed fine grey powder off his chest.

"Where is the amulet then, if she didn't take it?"

"You're brushing it off your chest," Erimenes said sourly.

Fost stared down at himself. The round burn on his chest ached, and it seemed to him to have the throb of permanence. On the black marble stone by his foot lay a leather thong charred in two.

"As I mentioned before, the Amulet of Living Flame had a finite amount of mystical energy stored in it. I feared it was near exhaustion, and I was right. You used the last of it in being restored to life." The spirit sniffed, as though he were about to cry. "The last! It could have gone to giving me that which I have longed for for so long, so long. And you took it, you great, stupid, selfish lout!"

"It was hardly my doing," Fost said defensively. Erimenes began to weep violently. The sound was so forlorn, Fost almost wished he had the amulet back so he could give it to the desolate shade.

Almost.

"Now, now, old ghost, cheer up. This hoodoo stone of yours has healed my lesser wounds as well as the greater. I'm ready to leave this worm-infested city. Will you come along?"

"Whatever would I wish to stay for?"

"This is your home. And of course your powers are greater here."

Erimenes made a rude noise. "Much good they did me. And what use are powers such as mine when they cannot serve to free me from this miserable jar? No, I'll come with you." His voice cheered noticeably. "I look forward to adventuring with you again, Fost, do you know? What do you intend now? To fare north through the Gate of the Mountains and sample the fleshpots of Kara-Est?"

"I fare north all right," Fost said. "But not to Kara-Est. Unless Moriana's trail leads me there."

"You follow the bitch to kill her?" Eagerness pulsed in the spirit's words.

Fost shook his head. "No. Not at all." He laughed a puzzled laugh. "I should hate her for what she did, Erimenes, and yet I don't. She murdered me but she thought she did the right thing." He laughed again, more loudly. "Maybe I don't feel bitter about it because it isn't permanent."

"Maybe she'll do a better job next time," Erimenes grumbled.

"Now, now, none of that." Fost sobered. "I want to warn her, Erimenes. She thinks she's got the Amulet of Living Flame and if she goes up against Synalon . . ." Fost paused, thinking. Finally he asked, "What does this Destiny Stone do anyway?"

"A mere trifle," Erimenes said. "Now let me tell you of the rich treasure troves that lie all around you."

"Think, Erimenes," Fost said. "Think how marvelous it will be. All the centuries of peace and quiet down here alone in the middle of this glacier, with nothing to disturb your meditations . . ."

"Very well," Erimenes said with ill grace. "It alters the luck of whoever wears it. Sometimes it works ill, sometimes good."

"It alternates, then?"

"No. There is no predicting the sequence, though many have tried. So it was that the Destiny Stone, though in ways immeasurably more powerful than the Amulet of Living Flame, was reckoned far less valuable."

"I see." Fost pondered what he'd learned. The Destiny Stone could enable Moriana to best Synalon at a stroke—or betray her to her sister's unimaginable revenge. There was no way to guess which.

Great Ultimate, I have to warn her! he thought. *Why?* asked a voice in his head. *She tried to kill you.*

She did kill you. Why do you care what becomes of her? When it comes to that, why not join with Synalon and gain your vengeance?

"Because I love her," he said aloud.

"The more fool you," said Erimenes.

"Yes," he said. "The more fool I." He hitched the strap of Erimenes's satchel over his shoulder. "Now, my nebulous friend, what's this you say about plunder? I'll do better pursuing our wayward princess if I've gold in my purse than if I go blundering about in my usual poverty-stricken manner."

Blood seeped into the ancient streets of Athalau. Blood congealed, blood froze. But somewhere beneath the ice blood still ran to the pumping of a heart.

When the ice block had fallen from above, a corner had struck the portico of the Palace. The ice did not lie flat on the street, nor had it entirely crushed the life from one who lay near the portico.

Like a wounded, pale animal, a hand emerged from beneath the upraised corner of the ice. Behind it dragged an arm. A second hand appeared, crushed and bloody. Between them the arms drew forth a body. Many bones were broken and much of its blood had seeped out to mingle with that of a half score of men, but that blood was the Blood Royal of the City in the Sky, and those of Etuul breed did not gracefully heed the Hell Call.

Prince Rann lived.